The woman was spectacular.

She was tall with a confident stride and economy of movement that spoke of power. Ty waited a beat for her partner to arrive, and then it settled over him that this woman had strode right into an unfamiliar watering hole alone, one with at least eight Harleys parked out front, and she had walked in with a self-assurance that showed either foolishness or strength.

Strength, he decided. That to him was more appealing than beauty because it took grit to survive up here. Both fortitude and compromise.

The tilt of her head and the way she scanned her surroundings gave her the air of a woman who knew what she was doing. There was no hesitation or wariness as she took in the bar. If he didn't know better, he'd say she owned the place.

BLACK ROCK GUARDIAN

JENNA KERNAN

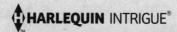

For Jim, always.

ISBN-13: 978-1-335-52643-4

Black Rock Guardian

Copyright © 2018 by Jeannette H. Monaco

Recycling programs
for this product may
not exist in your area.

Printed in U.S.A.

Jenna Kernan has penned over two dozen novels and received two RITA® Award nominations. Jenna is every bit as adventurous as her heroines. Her hobbies include recreational gold prospecting, scuba diving and gem hunting. Jenna grew up in the Catskills and currently lives in the Hudson Valley in New York State with her husband. Follow Jenna on Twitter, @jennakernan, on Facebook or at jennakernan.com.

Books by Jenna Kernan

Harlequin Intrigue

Apache Protectors: Wolf Den

Surrogate Escape
Tribal Blood
Undercover Scout
Black Rock Guardian

Apache Protectors: Tribal Thunder

Turquoise Guardian
Eagle Warrior
Firewolf
The Warrior's Way

Apache Protectors

Shadow Wolf
Hunter Moon
Tribal Law
Native Born

Harlequin Historical

Gold Rush Groom
The Texas Ranger's Daughter
Wild West Christmas
A Family for the Rancher
Running Wolf

Harlequin Nocturne

Dream Stalker
Ghost Stalker
Soul Whisperer
Beauty's Beast
The Vampire's Wolf
The Shifter's Choice

Visit the Author Profile page at Harlequin.com.

CAST OF CHARACTERS

Ty Redhorse—The former US Marine with gang affiliations is on the wrong side of the law again. Only this time it's not tribal police on his tail but the FBI.

FBI Field Agent Beth Hoosay—An undercover agent assigned to the Turquoise Canyon surrogate baby ring case. Her job is to infiltrate the tribe's gang and find all evidence necessary to prosecute the involved members. Her short list includes Ty Redhorse.

Dr. Kee Redhorse—The eldest of Ty's brothers and a physician who recently helped tribal police shut down illegal operations at the tribe's health clinic.

Field Agent Luke Forrest—FBI lieutenant heading the investigation of the missing girls on Turquoise Canyon Reservation.

Jake Redhorse—Ty's younger brother and a newly hired tribal police officer.

Lori Redhorse—Ty's new sister-in-law and a nurse at the tribe's health clinic.

Jack Bear Den—The tribe's senior detective.

Wallace Tinnin—Chief of the tribal police force.

Faras Pike—Leader of the tribe's only gang, the Wolf Posse.

Chino Aria—Gang muscle and protection for Faras Pike.

Quinton Ford—Faras's right-hand man.

Jewell Tasa—Faras's girl.

Vitoli Volkov—Russian mobster working for Leonard Usov and heading the surrogate operations on Turquoise Canyon.

Leonard Usov—Russian mobster for the Kuznetzov crime family with responsibilities for operations in the Southwest region.

Chapter One

At the sound of tires crunching on the gravel drive, Ty Redhorse glanced up from beneath the hood of the '76 Cadillac Eldorado to see two cop cars pull before the open bay of his garage. His heart sank as he straightened and came to attention, as if he was still in the US Marines. The tribal police vehicles rolled to a stop. Trouble, he thought, arriving on his doorstep.

They only had six men on the Turquoise Canyon force, and two of them were here at his shop. That did not bode well, and the fact that one of them was his younger brother only made things worse. He and Jake rarely spoke and when they did it usually ended badly. But Jake had been by yesterday and Ty had been touched to see how relieved Jakey was to see him alive and well. Small wonder after what Ty had been through.

Hemi, Ty's dog, had been even happier, showing her unrestrained joy at finding him again. Jake had Hemi out searching and she tracked him, but by then he'd already made it home to the rez and to Kee, who stitched him up. Wasn't easy because he'd lost a lot of blood.

Jake cast him a worried look and glanced at Ty's shoulder as he put his unit in Park. Clearly Kee had told him about the injury. Ty inclined his chin at Jake.

The little brother Ty had helped raise, and protect from the gang, had turned out fine. The late-day sun of an ordinary Friday afternoon in late October gilded Jake's skin, and the uniform gave him an air of respectability. Ty smiled, unable to resist indulging in the pride that rose in his chest at Jake inside his SUV.

The big man stepped from his police unit. That was Jack Bear Den, the tribe's only detective, since they'd rescinded the offer to hire detective Ava Hood. Now, there was a woman after his heart, breaking the law to get her niece back. Yes, her career had imploded, but Ty would bet she didn't regret a thing.

Bear Den took charge of the most important cases on the rez. And he was here. Ty's eyes narrowed. Not good.

"Hello, Ty," said Bear Den, extending his paw of a hand.

Ty glanced at the rag he held, knowing he could use it to wipe away the worst of the motor oil, but opted against it. He accepted Jack's hand and watched as realization dawned. Bear Den's clean palm was now slick with filthy brown motor oil. Ty's smile brightened. The day was looking up.

"This is a surprise. You boys need an oil change?" asked Ty.

Jack shook his head.

"Search my shop?" He motioned to the interior.

It wasn't really a joke. They'd done it before. But Ty's days of running a chop shop were over. He had mediated a position that allowed him to exist on the fringe of the tribe's gang, the Wolf Posse, which had helped him when no one else would. All that had changed when each of his brothers needed his help. Getting that help had been costly. And one, two, three, the gang had him again. Favors did not come free.

He was caught.

Bear Den held his smile as he kept his right hand well away from his spotless clothing.

"It's clean," said Ty, indicating the Cadillac with its hood up. "Even have the paperwork."

"I believe you," said the detective. "I saw the car you restored for the chief's boy, Gus. The detailing is amazing."

Ty's eyes narrowed at the flattery.

Jake was now making his way over. He, at least, knew not to block the bay doors with his vehicle. His little brother had the look of a man who wished to be anywhere but where he was. He came to a stop two steps behind the detective, making it clear who was in charge. Ty's gaze flicked to Jake's and he read stress in his brother's wrinkled brow. Jake did not think this would go well. Ty flicked his focus back to Bear Den.

"What can I do for the boys in blue?" Ty's hand went to his forearm and he rubbed his thumb over his skin where his gang tattoo sat below the one of the marine emblem that he'd had done when in the United States Marine Corps. When he realized what he was doing, he forced his hand to his side. The grease covered most of the ink anyway.

"We're here about our missing girls," said Bear Den.

Ty knew about the missing teenagers. Suspected he knew far more than Detective Bear Den.

Police had a crime, they needed a suspect. So what crime was Jack Bear Den interested in pinning on him?

"When you getting married to that Fed, Jack?" asked Ty, changing the subject and using the detective's first name with the desired result. Bear Den's face flushed. "She's an explosives expert, right? Should make life interesting."

Bear Den did not take the bait, but he shifted from one foot to the other. Ty had him off balance.

Bear Den glanced to Jake, who stepped alongside his superior, hands on hips, as if he even had the least control of his oldest brother. Jake had two years of community college and had passed the test and joined the force right after graduation. But he'd never joined the Marine Corps or seen the kind of horrors both Ty and his youngest brother, Colt, had witnessed. Thank God.

Maybe that was why Jake felt comfortable with a gun strapped to his hip while Ty had had his fill of them in the marines.

To Jake there was right and there was wrong. That must be so comforting, not to be bothered with all those shades of gray. But who had Jake called when he realized that little white newborn he had already fallen in love with was in danger? Not the tribal police force.

"We have reason to believe that the Wolf Posse is responsible for the selection of the women that the Russian mob is targeting," said Bear Den. "Our women."

"Girls, wouldn't you say?" said Ty. "What I hear, not one is over nineteen and Maggie Kesselman's only fourteen. Right?"

Ty folded his arms, the grease on his palms sliding easily around his formidable biceps.

"You didn't deny gang involvement," said Bear Den.

"What tipped you off, Minnie Cobb attacking the health clinic, or Earle Glass trying to snatch Kacey Doka back?" Ty asked, naming the two gang members now in custody. The gang had already written them off, so no risk of revealing new information there. "Or maybe it was my big brother, Kee, helping you find that kidnapped detective on loan. What was her name? Detective Hood, right? Way I hear it, Kee has a new girlfriend and you got a new dispatcher. How does Carol Dorset feel about that?" he asked, mentioning the woman who had held the position since before Ty was born.

Bear Den scowled and his gaze shifted to Ty's injured shoulder.

Ty resisted the urge to test the stitches. Kee had put them in himself two days ago after Ty managed to make it the twenty odd miles from Antelope Lake to the rez. Once he was back on tribal land, the Feds could not touch him. So they'd sent Bear Den to rattle his cage.

Ty gave in and scratched his left shoulder. The stitches were beginning to itch.

Jake's face flushed and he pressed his lips between his teeth, clearly unhappy to be placed between his idol and his embarrassment of a brother. His worried expression, as he braced for what Ty would do next, just burned Ty up. Afraid he'd have to arrest him, probably. Ty would like to see him try.

His brother seemed to have put on weight since he'd married Lori Mott, but Ty knew he could still take him because Jake and Kee both fought fair, while he and his youngest brother, Colt, fought to win.

"So, you boys have any idea what will happen to me if one of the Wolf Posse drives by and sees two cop cars parked at my shop?" asked Ty.

"I'd imagine it would be easier to explain than if I haul your ass into the station as an accessory to kidnapping," said Bear Den.

Bear Den was talking about Ty transporting Colt's girl, Kacey, off the rez and back to her captors two and a half weeks ago. Not kidnapping, but darn close, and he was sure the tribal police would not appreciate the subtle differences. He was in serious risk of the tribe bringing charges against him, possibly turning the case over to the attorney general, and Bear Den was all for that.

"Shouldn't you be chasing the guys that blew up our dam?" asked Ty.

Bear Den's mouth quirked. "I'm multitasking. Now, you want to talk to us here or there?"

Ty faced off against the big man. He knew he could not take Bear Den in a fair fight, but he had a length of pipe just inside the open bay door. "What do you want, exactly?"

"Just some help," said Jake, standing with palms out. "These are our girls that they're taking. We want them back."

Ty had no objections to that. He just didn't want to stop breathing because of it. "What's that got to do with me?"

Bear Den took over again. His hair was growing out and it curled like a pig's tail at his temples. Ty wondered again just who had fathered this monster of a man. Certainly not Mr. Bear Den, who was big but not supersized.

"No secret you're in the Posse." Bear Den pointed to the grease-smeared tattoo of four feathers forming a *W* for wolf on Ty's forearm. The gang was an all-Native branch of the Three Kings, wore the yellow and black colors of that group and had adopted an indigenous symbol that resembled the crown worn by the Kings while representing their Native culture.

"I'm retired."

"No such thing," said Bear Den.

True enough. A better word would have been *inactive*. He knew more than he would like and less than he used to, which was still too much. And he owed favors. Way too many favors.

Ty no longer did their dirty work, but he looked

the other way. Kept their cars running smoother and faster than law-enforcement vehicles and drove the occasional errand. He did what was necessary. There was just no other way to survive in a brotherhood of wolves.

"We need to know how they choose the targets, if they have targeted anyone else and where the missing are being held."

Ty could never find out that last one because the gang only snatched and delivered. They did not store the taken. That was the Kuznetsov crime family, a Russian mob that dealt in women the way a farmer deals in livestock. Buy. Sell. Breed. And they were just one of many. The outer thread of a network that stretched around the world.

"Is that all?" asked Ty, and smirked.

Bear Den's frown deepened. The man was aching to arrest him, but the tribal council had voted against turning Ty over to the Feds after the incident with Kacey Doka because her statement included that she had wished to be returned to her captors and that she accepted a ride from Ty. In other words, no coercion or capture, so not kidnapping. Ty suspected the fact that he was walking around free burned the detective's butt.

"That would do it," said Bear Den.

Ty leaned back against the grill of the Caddy and folded his arms, throwing up the first barricade. "I don't know if they have more targets. I don't know where the missing are being held and I don't know how they choose."

"But you could find out," said Jake.

Ty gave his brother a look of regret.

"Help them, like you helped me," whispered Jake as he extended his right hand, reaching out to his big brother from across a gap too wide for either of them to cross.

"You're family, Jakey. It's different." He thrust a hand into his jeans, feeling the paper with the address of the meet in his pocket. Ty rubbed the note between his thumb and index finger. "Listen, guys, I have a nice honest business here. So how about this, how about you do your job instead of asking me to do it?"

Bear Den glanced at his garage and the car beyond the Caddy.

"It's all legit, Bear Den. You can't get to me that way."

Bear Den snorted like a bull. "If they ask you for details on our investigation, could you feed them some false information?"

"They kill people for that."

Judging from his expression, that eventuality did not seem to bother the detective in the least.

"Bear Den, your police force arrested me and you did everything you could to get the tribe to turn me over to the Feds. I owe you, but not a favor."

"You threatening me?" asked the detective.

"That would be illegal. I am telling you, nicely, to piss off."

"We'd like you to meet someone," said Jake.

"Not happening."

"She's FBI," said Jake.

Ty laughed. "Oh, then let me rephrase. Not happening, ever."

Chapter Two

FBI field agent Beth Hoosay sat in the silver F-150 pickup with tribal police officer Jake Redhorse, waiting for full dark. Redhorse had parked across the highway and out of sight, but with a clear view of the roadside bar favored by bikers and Jake's older brother, Ty Redhorse. In the bed of the truck was her motorcycle, prepped and ready.

Earlier in the day, the tribal police detective, Jack Bear Den, had tried and failed to get Ty to meet with her. So they would do it the hard way.

It was beyond Beth's comprehension why the Turquoise Canyon Apache tribe's leadership had voted to keep Ty on the reservation instead of turning him over to the authorities for trial. And he was walking around free.

That was about to change, in twelve hours to be exact. Because Beth was about to meet Ty on his own turf tonight and with the advantage of him not knowing who and what she was. She had backup, but she did not intend to need it. The agents could hear everything she said and had eyes on her outside the roadside bar. Once she was inside, it would be audio only because Beth insisted that the other agents would never blend in a place like this. They'd be spotted as outsiders instantly.

She, on the other hand, had been in this joint once before when she was younger and more rebellious, after her dad had died, and she'd had the gall to date a guy who owned a bike. Worse still, he had taught her to ride. She was grateful for that much. The rest of their relationship had been less positive because it seemed to her that he'd wanted her only as an accessory to his chopper. Her mother said the bike would be the death of her and that the guy had been interested only because of her unique looks, which blended Native heritage with her father's Caribbean roots, and made her seem exotic to the son of a soybean farmer. Sometimes she just wanted to blend in. But today her looks were an asset and the reason she was here.

Beth had been handpicked for this assignment because she was Apache on her mother's side. Not Tonto Apache, like Ty Redhorse. Her Native ancestry came from the line that fought with Geronimo and lost, which was why her reservation was up in Oklahoma instead of here, where they had lost to the US Army with the help of this very tribe. She tried not to let it bother her, but many on her rez still thought the Tonto Apache were more desert people who could not even understand their language. They spoke a language that only they and God could understand.

Beth didn't care about old grudges. She cared

about having a rare and shining opportunity to make a big case. The possibilities were so enthralling they made her chest ache. She wanted this, wanted the respect and acclaim that came with a bust of this importance.

Another truck pulled into the lot and a lone driver slid out and hiked up his jeans before slamming the truck door. The parking area was nearly full. They did good business on any Friday night, and tonight was no exception. Many of the men inside were just coming from work and others had no work but arrived when the bar was most crowded. She knew the establishment was most busy between five and eight and closed at midnight, except on weekends, when the place closed at two in the morning. It was approaching eight and she was beginning to worry that Ty might not show.

"He's usually here by now," said Jake. His voice sounded hopeful. "Maybe I should go in with you. It's a rough place."

"I don't need an escort, patrolman." She let him know with her tone just what she thought of his advice. Showing up with a police officer that everyone here knew was a terrible idea.

Beth had plans. She would investigate the missing women, tie their disappearances to the Kuznetsov crime family and make the kind of case that got a person noticed in the Bureau, and with that notice came the kind of posting Beth craved. Truth be told, she didn't like Oklahoma or the field office in Oklahoma City, known for the bombing of the federal building.

She wanted a major posting with status in a place far away from the flat, windy plains. Unlike the army, the FBI measured rank with cases, postings and a title. So she set her sights on a major case, a major posting in a major office. The plan was to run a field office before she hit thirty-five. And Ty Redhorse could get on board or get out of her way, preferably in a small prison cell in Phoenix.

"That's him," said Jake, slumping down in his seat.

Beth smiled as Ty Redhorse roared into the dirt lot on a cream-and-coffee-colored motorcycle. The sled was a beauty, a classic Harley from the nineties, all muscle and gleaming chrome. She could not keep back her appreciation. She admired power.

Beth and Jake sat in the dark tucked up against the closed feed store across from the watering hole. Behind them, her guys sat in a van, their view blocked until Jake took off.

Ty had worked all day in his auto body shop according to surveillance. He had given no sign that his left shoulder had been recently ripped open while he was crashing through a picture window in a home in Antelope Lake. But that was the story his oldest brother, Kee, had told.

The man in question was trim and muscular and wore no helmet. He rolled to a stop right before the bar, as if he owned it, and Beth wondered if that space was reserved for him. His chopper fit perfectly between the black trucks that she knew belonged to members of the Wolf Posse, the tribe's one and only gang. Ty cut the engine, and the world went quiet.

Then he planted his booted feet on both sides of his beautiful bike and rocked it to the stand as if it weighed nothing at all.

His driving gloves ended at his palms, giving her a flashing view of fingers raking through his shoulder-length black hair. He wore it blunt-cut in a traditional style so old she did not even know where it originated. The wind had done a job tousling his hair and he took a moment to set it right, raking his fingers back over his scalp. Then he threw a leg over the seat and dismounted the bike like a cowboy coming in off the range. He glanced around and looked right in their direction, gazing at them for a minute. Beside her, Jake held his breath and scooted lower in his seat.

"He can see us," whispered Officer Redhorse, more to himself, she thought, than her.

"Not unless he has night-vision goggles," she said, not whispering. He'd have to be some kind of jackrabbit to hear her from clear across the road. But she could hear him, thanks to the setup from the tech guys.

His gaze flicked away to a teen who was straddling an expensive new mountain bicycle that was, of course, black. On the boy's head sat a yellow ball cap, sideways, bill flat. He wore a new oversized black satin sports jacket. Beth made him for about thirteen because of his size. The gang colors were yellow and black, and Beth knew that recruitment started early. Ty went over to him.

"Who's that?" she asked Jake.

"Randy Tasa. Lives up in Koun'nde. He's in the ninth grade."

"Long bike ride."

"His sister, Jewell, is probably inside. She's Faras's girl."

Faras Pike was the current head of the Wolf Posse and one of the targets of her investigation.

Beth lifted the cone so she could hear them.

"Whatcha doing out here so late, Randy?" Ty asked. His voice was deeper than his brother's and held a dangerous edge.

"Deliveries."

Deliveries, my ass, thought Beth. The boy was selling weed to the customers. He was too young to get anything but a slap on the wrist, making him the perfect pusher for the gang.

"Let me see," ordered Ty.

The boy obediently reached into his coat and showed Ty the freezer bag filled with what Beth believed to be smaller baggies of weed.

"You make any money?" asked Ty.

"Some."

"Give it to me."

Was he actually shaking down a child?

"I'm supposed to give it to Chino."

"Did I ask you what you were supposed to do?"

The boy held out an envelope. Ty snatched it from him, took the weed and then took his cap. "This bag is light, Randy."

"No. I swear."

"Light," he repeated. "I'm telling Faras that you're a thief."

"No." Randy was crying now. "He'll kill me."

"He doesn't kill children. Run home, Randy, and don't come back or I'll put a cap in your ass."

Randy wiped his nose and Ty took one menacing step toward the boy, grabbing the handlebars of the new bike. "I said *run*."

The boy sprang from the seat and ran as fast as his sticklike legs would carry him. He was too young to be hanging around a bar. But not too young to have his services bought for a ball cap and a new bike. Ty might have done the boy a favor.

Beth pushed aside that thought.

Jake shifted in his seat. Yeah, she'd be uncomfortable, too, if this gem of humanity was her big brother. Luckily, she had no siblings and was free as a bird. She could pack everything she needed in the saddlebags of her bike and head to LA, DC or NY. But first she had to make a big case. Would her mother even notice she was gone?

Ty let the bike fall and headed for the door of the bar, carrying the weed in his leather bomber jacket, which was black, of course. Jake insisted that his brother operated on the fringes of the gang. Jake said that Ty's responsibility was only to keep the gang's cars running. All evidence pointed to the contrary.

He had enough weed on him right now for her to get a conviction, but since he was on the rez, arresting him would just get her in hot water with Lieutenant Luke Forrest, who headed this operation. She reported to him, for now. So she watched Ty walk away and ignored the bad taste in her mouth. If she got a break, she'd catch Ty Redhorse with something far more serious than a bag of weed. She didn't expect to get that lucky. Most of her luck came from hard work and taking the occasional risk.

She reached for the door release.

"Wait," she ordered Redhorse. "Don't leave unless you see me leave with your brother. Then follow us."

Beth had dressed in clothing that showed she was a woman but also concealed her high-performance liquid chromatography, abbreviated as HPLC and commonly known as pepper spray, her service weapon and handcuffs. On her right hand she wore a series of carefully selected rings designed to inflict maximum damage and lacerate skin should she have to throw a punch.

What she intended was to charm and pick up Ty Redhorse in front of all his buddies on his home turf. Tomorrow, well after all the customers in this watering hole had assumed that he'd made a successful score, Beth would let him know who and what she actually was. She suspected that Ty did not want Faras Pike, the leader of the posse, to know what he had done to help his older brother, Kee, and that he was on less than stable ground with the gang. A little more shaking might just get him on their side.

Risk and reward, she thought, and slid from the truck and onto the packed dirt parking area.

"Help me get my sled down," she said.

Jake lowered the back gate and set the metal ramp.

Because of the intentionally disabled starter motor, Beth needed to bump-start her motorcycle. She released the straps holding her bike and mounted the seat, then rolled it down the ramp in second, using the incline to get it going fast enough to allow the engine to engage.

She roared across the street, anticipating Ty's face tomorrow morning at eight, when he saw her walk into the interrogation room. Between now and then, she intended to find out everything she could about the second-oldest Redhorse brother.

Chapter Three

Ty walked into the roadhouse and glanced about. The mix of the usual patrons filled the stools surrounding the rectangular bar, which had seating all the way around except for the hinged portion that allowed the help in and out.

Beyond the center altar to drinking was the stage, which rose a good sixteen inches above the floor level but was dark because the musical entertainment didn't begin until nine. By then most of these men—working men—would be home with their families. They just needed a short transition between one and the other.

There were exceptions—men who were not drinking after work because they were still on the job. The first, Quinton Ford, sat on a bar stool. Quinton was lanky with close-cropped black hair and a hawkish face that bore acne scars on his gaunt cheeks. One hand rested in his open jacket as he used the half-lowered zipper like a sling. Ty knew his hand was on the grip of a pistol. Quinton faced the door with the other hand on his untouched beer. His eyes met

Ty's, and Ty nodded to Faras Pike's man. Quinton raised his chin in acknowledgment and then his gaze flicked back to the door.

Ty was no threat to Faras Pike.

There were tables to the left and everyone knew the ones under the wall of highway signs, stolen from all over the state, were reserved for Wolf Posse members. There at his usual spot was Faras Pike, the leader of the tribe's gang. Perched on his knee was his current favorite, Jewell Tasa.

Jewell wore a glittery sequined gold crop top that featured an unobstructed view of her midriff, which was tight and toned. Jewell's skinny jeans and biker boots made her a shimmering billboard of gang colors. Her makeup was thick, ringing her eyes like a raccoon, and her long black hair had been bleached blond at the tips.

Faras spotted Ty before Jewell did, and lifted her from his lap. Then he gave her rump an affectionate pat to send her off to the group of women at the nearby table. She spotted Ty and sauntered past him, hips swaying as if advertising what he could not have.

The unattached women at the table gave Ty encouraging smiles. He was not interested in more entanglements with the gang, no matter how tight they wore their clothing. So he turned his attention to Faras.

The head of the Wolf Posse was small with a face that had been handsome once, but the smoking, drinking and responsibilities of his position weighed heavily on that face and Faras now looked like a man nearing forty, instead of twenty-eight. His hair was drawn back in a single braid and he wore a hoodie, jeans, cowboy boots that were all black and several thick gold chains around his neck. His take on the black-and-gold color scheme. His ears were pierced and he wore diamond studs in each that Ty very much feared were real.

Seated between him and the bar was his second man, Chino Aria, his newest favored muscle. Chino could handle most situations if he didn't have to think or make any decision on his feet. Chino's appeal came from his size and bulk. The tattoos on his neck and bald head helped discourage trouble.

Ty cut a direct path for the two men.

"S'up, bro?" said Faras as he came to a stop before the circular booth and table.

"That little shit, Randy Tasa, is stealing your stash, is what's up," said Ty. He slid into the vinyl seat beside Faras. Chasing off Randy was a risk, because his big sister, Jewell, was already in the Wolf Posse and becoming Faras's favorite.

Chino looked none too happy at Ty's appearance, judging from the way his mouth tugged down on his broad jowly face.

"Randy Tasa? He don't work for me." Faras snapped his fingers before Chino's face, redirecting his stare from Ty to Faras. "Chino, we recruit Tasa?"

"Yeah," said Chino.

"When were you going to mention it?"

"First night, boss. Wanted to see how he worked out."

Ty scowled. You didn't earn a bike like that in one

night. Chino was lying and Ty wondered why. It occurred to him that Randy would make a very good spy, keeping an eye on his big sister's business. But that was the sort of thing he'd expect Faras to pull. Perhaps he'd underestimated Chino?

Chino laid his beefy fists on the table, challenging Ty with his stare. Ty set the bag of weed on the padded bench between him and Faras.

"Yo, don't bring that in here," said Faras, sliding away.

"He was smoking the product instead of making sales. You get him that bike?"

Faras lifted a brow at Chino, who nodded. Faras glared. He knew how to recruit kids into the gang. Up until this minute, Ty thought the decision of when and who was recruited had rested solely with Faras. From the way he was glaring at Chino, perhaps Faras did as well.

"You picked it?" asked Faras.

Chino nodded.

Ty broke in. "Well, he tried to sell it to me for fifty bucks."

"That little puke," said Chino, coming awake. Unfortunately, he forgot he was sitting in a booth and so, when he stood, the bench did not move back and he collided with the table, sending their beer bottles sloshing to their sides.

Faras swore.

"Sorry, boss."

Chino used his sleeve to prevent the river of beer from reaching Faras's lap.

Ty tossed Randy's cap onto the puddle of beer. "I took his bike. It's out front."

Faras sighed and lifted a finger to Sancho, the head barkeeper, who was always very attentive to Faras, met his gaze and pointed to the spilled beer. One of the bartenders was out from behind the hinged counter and mopping up before Chino had even sat his big fat butt back down.

"I'll need to find a replacement," said Faras. "Deliveries, you know."

Ty knew there was no stopping that. But Randy had a future. He was a runner. A good one. If he was smart and lucky, he might just run out of Turquoise Canyon and make a life that did not involve allegiances to the posse. One little minnow, escaping the net. Ty felt a longing for a freedom from such allegiances, or at least to become something other than the family poster boy for wasted potential. He wasn't the only one who thought so.

Kee had been asked to join the Turquoise Guardians right out of med school, as if it was a foregone conclusion. Gaining admission to the tribe's medicine society was a coup that Ty coveted. But to be asked to join Tribal Thunder, the warrior sect of that medicine society, well, that was an honor above all others. Last month, they'd asked Jake to join.

"Chino, get rid of this and get me another beer," said Faras.

His man grabbed the baggie Faras pushed at him

under the table, tucked it into his jacket and slid out of the booth. Then he hurried to the bar.

Faras waited until Chino and the bartender both retreated.

"You can't keep doing this," said Faras.

Ty said nothing.

"It costs me money and time."

Ty met his gaze and read the warning there. Things were serious now. With the pressure of the Russians and the tribal police bringing in the FBI, Faras was in a difficult spot. He could not afford to bring his suppliers less, to even let one little fish swim out of the net.

"That's the last one. You feel me?" said Faras.

Ty nodded.

"And where you been? I've been trying to reach you since Tuesday. You don't answer your phone or return my calls."

Ty told himself not to move his healing shoulder. Not to give away that he'd been injured, running for his life in the woods, trying to reach the reservation and home before the Feds caught him and locked him up beside his dad. Because if Faras knew, he'd also know that Ty followed his brother to the holding house that was stop one in the surrogate operation.

"I had a delivery in Phoenix. That '78 Nova. Matte-black."

"Phoenix and back takes six hours."

Ty met his gaze without shifting in his seat or offering further explanation.

Faras dragged his hand down his braid, tugged and

then tossed it over his shoulder. "Listen, you asked me for a favor. You asked me to lie to my suppliers about a certain baby girl dying. I did that."

"And you already called that favor. Sent me on a pickup. I drove Kacey Doka at your request and I delivered her, didn't I?"

"And both those guys are dead."

"How you figure that's my fault?"

"It's your brother's fault. Colt killed them."

"He's not a dog on a leash. He loves Kacey."

"Love? Don't make me laugh. How did Colt know where to find those Russian dudes?"

"Dunno. Followed me?"

"You better hope that's how it went. If you tipped him…" Faras sat back in the booth and looked at the ceiling. Then dragged in a long breath and exhaled.

Ty read the signs. Now he was already in the danger zone. He regretted chasing off Randy. The timing had been bad.

Faras met his gaze across the table, his eyes flat and cold. "You still owe me for the baby. I'm calling it in. Moving you to transport."

"I delivered Kacey. That covers it."

"Not hardly. Two more of Vitoli's guys were killed in Antelope Lake."

"Too bad." Ty tried and failed to look sorry. The bastards had nearly killed Kee.

"And you were there."

"No."

"Says you."

Faras didn't know. He was fishing, putting together the pieces.

"No way," said Ty.

"Just making a three-day delivery of a Chevy Nova. Yeah, I heard. You want that baby to stay dead?"

Ty felt trapped. His entire life he'd been trapped. By his father, by the Marine Corps, by the gang. All he wanted in this shitty world was to have the chance, like Kee and Jake and Colt, to make something of himself. But he'd made his bed at eighteen. He didn't regret what he had done. But he never anticipated that by accepting Faras's help back then he would be tied to the man forever and painted with the same broad brush.

He wanted out. But if he left, just got on his bike and rode, who would protect his family from these predators that lived inside their rez like a nest of vipers?

The police couldn't do it, because they had laws to follow and they were outmatched in numbers and finances. The Feds couldn't do it. They didn't operate here unless invited and they flitted in and out like migrating birds while he wallowed down here in the mud.

"You hear me, Ty?" said Faras.

Ty nodded.

Faras leaned in. "I got a new operation. We're cookin' now. Ice."

Ty frowned, hating crystal meth and hating even

more that the posse would be in production on his rez. "That so?"

"Yeah. First lab is in production up on Deer Kill Meadow Road. Old hay barn up there."

"Won't someone see the smoke?"

"Nights only. You gonna start transport next week."

The hell he was. "Sure."

Chino returned with the beer. Ty left his on the table, went to the bar and sat beside Quinton. Ty was sitting facing the taps when Quinton's foot dropped heavily off the bar stool as he sat forward. He did not reach for his gun, but his eyes widened and he looked as if someone had thrown a bucket of cold water in his face.

Ty spun on the swivel stool toward the door. A woman paused on the Budweiser floor runner and glanced about. Ty thought her attention paused on him, but that might have been wishful thinking.

"Damn," said Quinton. "Why I have to be working when something like that shows up?"

Ty thought it was a *someone*, not a *something*. But he agreed with Quinton that the woman was spectacular. She was tall with a confident stride and an economy of movement that spoke of power. Ty waited a beat for her partner to arrive and then it settled over him that this woman had come by herself to an unfamiliar watering hole, one with at least eight Harleys parked out front, and she had walked in with a self-assurance that showed either foolishness or strength.

Strength, he decided. That to him was more appealing than beauty because it took grit to survive up here. Both fortitude and compromise.

The tilt of her head and the way she scanned her surroundings gave her the air of a woman who knew what she was doing. There was no hesitation or wariness as she took in her surroundings. If he didn't know better, he'd say she owned the place.

The conversation lulled as one after another of both the single and married men considered their chances. Several of the men turned back to their beers, taking themselves out of the race by fidelity to their mates, or just by judging themselves to be farm-league players in a major league game.

Ty leaned forward and drank her in like water. High brown suede boots, with silver studs around each ankle, hugged her well-defined calves. Her jeans were dark, new-looking and tight, showing legs that went on and on. The cropped leather jacket seemed to have lived a long, interesting life as a favorite garment, and Ty resented the way it hugged her upper body and breasts. Below the bottom of the jacket was a wide silver rodeo buckle, the kind that was won, not purchased. From here, it looked like the lady was a world-class barrel racer. Oh, how he would love to see her ride.

Her fawn-brown skin held the luster of gold undertones, catching the light on her high cheekbones. She seemed multiracial. He thought he recognized the Native American lineage in her distinctive facial structure. Her pale eyes hinted at European roots, and she had full lips, light brown skin and a curl of her brown shoulder-length hair. A natural beauty.

Women, sitting beside their men, placed proprietary hands on their companions, claiming them as she again swept the room with a slow scan. Her gaze fell on him. Her mouth quirked and he saw trouble coming his way, again. Only this time he felt like walking out to meet it.

She raised her voice to be heard above the jukebox as she kept her eyes fixed on his. "I'm looking for Ty Redhorse."

Chapter Four

In Beth's opinion, the photos of Ty Redhorse did not do him justice. They didn't capture his roguish grin or his speculative stare. His mug shot, taken when he was just seventeen, showed a scared kid, and the one furnished by his brother pictured a man posing with his family as if he was uncomfortable in his own skin.

Maybe he was just uncomfortable with his family. Must be awkward at Sunday supper with his two remaining brothers. Comparisons were inevitable.

This man was broad-shouldered with a slim athletic frame. He also had the devil-may-care smile of a pirate. His forehead was broad and smooth, making him look more like twenty-one instead of twenty-eight. There was a slight, shallow cleft in his chin. One of his eyebrows lifted in conjecture. Dark eyes met hers and set off a flutter low and deep inside her.

She ignored the warning and continued on. Nerves, she told herself as she moved toward him. She might find Ty physically attractive, but he was just her admission ticket to the Wolf Posse, a means to an end.

So it didn't matter how appealing she found his face and body. Beth liked bad boys, just not this one.

Still, there was something about him that made her regret the missed opportunity he presented. In another time and place she might have acted on impulse. But not now with so much on the line.

Beth had met his brother, Jake Redhorse, a rookie tribal officer, and had none of this immediate attraction. His younger brother had a look that she would describe as brooding. From the family photo, she thought the oldest brother, Kee, radiated the stability of a professional man with none of the indescribable edge of danger she found tempting. Unlike his oldest brother, this Redhorse man had none of that serious, stable aura. She knew of his youngest brother, Colt, only via computer records. Colt shared some of the defiant disregard she read in Ty's expression. But he also had PTSD and had given up speaking for months. That was way too much for her to ever want to take on. She met Ty's inquisitive stare. Everything about Ty seemed to broadcast mischief and the invitation to forget the rules and play.

"I'm Ty," he said.

All heads turned in his direction and then boomeranged back to her.

Beth had not anticipated the relaxed confidence of his physical self. He sat neither at attention nor slumped. Instead, he looked like he knew she was a problem heading toward him and he welcomed the diversion.

She used her thumb to adjust one of the rings on

her right hand, breaking the steady stare. The man to his left was Quinton Ford, one of the Wolf Posse's higher-ups. Ty sat right beside the gang's right-hand man.

How cozy, she thought.

He rose to his feet in an easy glide, his movements as relaxed as his expression. But his eyes glittered a warning that belied the ready smile. "What can I do for you?"

"I've got bike trouble. The owner of the diner said you were the man to see and he told me that I would find you here." She extended her hand. "I'm Beth."

He looked at her hand as if inspecting it and then his gaze flicked to her left hand. Was he searching for a ring on that all-important finger? Or the indentation and lighter skin that showed there had been one there recently? She wasn't sure, but there was a hesitation before his palm slid along hers in a sensual glide that made her skin pucker all over. His hand was clean, calloused. His nails showed the stain of stubborn motor oil. He gripped her hand and did not shake so much as stroke, his thumb caressing the sensitive skin on the back of her hand. Her heartbeat kicked up a notch and her lungs suddenly demanded more oxygen.

"Nice to meet you, Beth."

She drew back her hand, but it continued to tingle as if she'd just touched an electrified livestock fence.

"If you need a bike fixed," said Quinton Ford, interrupting, "you should ask Chino." He thumbed at the mountainous man sitting with the leader of the Wolf Posse.

"That so?" said Beth. "Why's that?"

"It's his specialty. Ty's is cars."

"A motor is a motor," said Beth. "And I don't think that Nathan would steer me wrong. What do *you* say, Ty?"

His smile relayed anticipation and mischief. "Let's have a look."

The whole point of coming here was to have everyone on his home turf see her leave with Ty and make the obvious conclusions. Her story to her supervisor, Luke Forrest, about getting a read on Ty was nonsense. She didn't need a read. All she ever wanted or needed to know about Ty Redhorse she'd found in his FBI file. What she desired was traction, an inescapable hook to get him on board, because he'd already turned down the Bureau's offer presented by his tribe.

If tomorrow morning, he discovered that he'd been seen leaving the roadside bar with an FBI field agent? Well, that was the sort of thing he might be inclined to want to keep to himself.

But Chino was on his way over. "I'll fix your bike," he said.

Beth had not anticipated a war over her sled. She definitely didn't want this mountainous wall of muscle to help her.

Ty stepped to intercept Chino Aria. "Lady asked for me."

"Because she doesn't know me," he said.

"And you're working," Ty reminded him.

Chino's expression went blank for a moment as his eyes lifted toward the ceiling. Then he glanced back at his boss, Faras Pike, who motioned to his muscle with two fingers.

"Master's calling," said Ty, just having to get a dig in, it seemed.

Not smart, thought Beth. If she wasn't undercover, she'd already have her hand on the grip of her pistol.

Chino shot Ty a glare that should have given him pause. Instead, it gave rise to a cocksure crooked smile that Beth admitted made her lips curl upward, as well. There was something satisfying about seeing the big man forced into retreat.

Chino pointed at Ty as if his finger was a gun. "Later," he said, and pulled the imaginary trigger.

Ty said nothing but scratched beside his mouth with his middle finger. Chino frowned and gave Ty one last angry look before he stalked away.

Ty motioned to the door. "Shall we?"

Beth swung her hips for all she was worth as she sauntered toward the exit. Just before leaving she grabbed Ty by the front of his black T-shirt and tugged. The kiss came naturally.

That surprised her. She'd thought it would feel forced. Unfortunately, they fit together all too well. Ty's mouth was hungry. His hands moved down her arms to capture her waist and tug. She did not resist, falling against him as he deepened the kiss.

She barely registered the hoots and banging from the customers, who all had ringside seats, as she'd intended. Beth closed her eyes and savored the velvety contact of his mouth and the sandy stubble of his cheek. She hadn't been really kissed in so long she had forgotten what it felt like.

As his tongue slid along hers and her body began to tingle in all the right places, she realized that she'd never been kissed like this. The warning bells sounded too late. She'd made a mistake, a costly one, because her body did not understand that this was work.

Beth broke away and saw that she'd wiped the crooked smile off Ty's face. He was now looking at her with a mixture of anticipation and healthy wariness. All large predators had that instinct—the ability to judge if he was facing an opportunity or a threat.

Ty reached past her and pushed open the door. The roar of the customers mixed with shouts of encouragement.

Someone shouted after them. "Fix that bike, Ty!"

Beth turned but not before she saw Ty wave to the crowd like the victor of some sporting competition. Beth smiled. He thought he'd won, but she believed that, in the interrogation room of his tribe's police station, when she flashed her badge, he might see things differently.

Chapter Five

Outside, the world was dark except for the single spotlight fixed above the bar, illuminating the rutted dirt parking area before the roadhouse. In the windows, the neon glow of beer advertising sent beams of bright color reflecting off the windshields of dusty pickup trucks.

"I'm this way," she said, leading him to the darkest portion of the lot.

Ty dragged her between two trucks and kissed her again. This time she did not kiss him for show. Oh, no, this time she let herself enjoy each nerve-tingling second. But when his hand moved from her lower back to her backside, she stepped away.

"The bike?" she reminded him.

"Yeah, but I'm figuring that if I fix it, you might use it to get away."

She smiled at him. He really was a handsome man. Such a shame he'd chosen so poorly in life. Those dark eyes gleamed with the promise of pleasure, and his mouth turned up in a way that offered a challenge she was tempted to accept. It was a winning combination. Especially when coupled with the hard jaw-line, straight nose and dark, slashing eyebrows. His hair was a windblown mess, as if he didn't care how it looked or, perhaps, understood that his mop of hair begged a woman to comb her fingers through the tangles. She indulged herself in the impulse as her eyes feasted on the quintessential bad boy.

The tribe should make warning posters about this one. Still, she was tempted. So tempted to see what he had.

"You need a shave," she said. His hair was as thick as a horse's tail. She drew her hand back and touched her own cheek. "You're giving me razor burn."

"I have a razor at my place," he said.

The man did not waste time.

"Unfortunately, I can't ride there. My bike…" She offered him a regretful look, but her eyes offered something else.

"Let's go see."

She led the way across the rutted, dusty lot. He fell into step just behind her left shoulder.

"What kind of sled you have?"

"It's a BMW F800GT."

He whistled as his hand stroked her bike, starting at the leather saddle and gliding all the way up to the instruments until his long fingers finally wrapped around one grip.

Beth shivered in response to that sensual glide, and he hadn't even touched her.

"Rich," he said. He stretched out his fingers and then wiped his hand across his flat stomach.

Beth's skin flushed and she found she needed a long intake of air. "I got it used off a guy who…well, he gave me a good price." She let him wonder about that. The bike was truly hers. She had purchased it at a police auction and knew it had been owned by a man who liked to gamble with his clients' money. The way she figured it, a bike like this deserved a better owner.

She'd parked it at an angle so no one parked too close and so she could push it out, if necessary.

"You rode in here?" asked Ty, turning his attention to the bike.

"Yeah. It died at the diner. So I checked what I could and then did a push-start. Lucky the diner is on a hill. Got it going all right."

Ty looked at the bike. "Battery, maybe."

"It's fine. Nearly new."

"You might have left the headlight on when you were in the diner."

She flipped on the headlight, which glowed brightly.

She pointed to the console. "Says it's good, plus I flipped back the saddle and tested one of the terminals to ground. It arced just fine."

"Gas?" he asked.

She cut her gaze away. "Please."

"So I won't ask if the kickstand was up and the sled in Neutral."

"You try and start it," she said.

He straddled the bike. She couldn't believe it, but he looked even more handsome. The neon glow from the beer signs illuminated his high cheekbones, and a lock of hair fell over his forehead as he tried and failed to get the bike started.

"How are the plugs?" he asked.

"Good, I think."

"Well, then I'd say you have gunk in the fuel lines. Maybe the clutch starter. Bike needs air, fuel and spark. We know you have spark and fuel, so…"

She swore as if surprised it was not a quick repair.

"Did the guy at the diner mention that I have a garage?"

Beth nodded.

"I live above my garage."

Which she knew, but it was obvious he wanted her to know where the closest bed might be.

"You want me to bring it tomorrow morning?"

"Now is good." He gestured with his thumb over his shoulder. "Only thing, you'll have to drive. I already had too much to drink."

Which was interesting because she knew from Jake that Ty Redhorse did not drink.

"I don't think I want a drunk working on my bike."

"I could fix a carburetor drunk or asleep."

"Nobody drives my bike."

He slid back on the seat. "You want me to bump-start the bike with you on the back?"

He wiggled his eyebrows and she accepted the challenge.

"What about your bike?" she asked.

"In good hands."

No one would touch his bike. He had the protection

of the Wolf Posse and tribal police, since his brother was on the force.

"Just out of curiosity, how were you planning to get home?"

"I never plan that far ahead," said Ty.

"You don't look or act or smell drunk," said Beth.

"Maybe I just can't resist lying flat across your back or maybe I want to see what an eight-hundred-cc in-line engine feels like. It's a tour bike. Plenty of room."

"If you fix my bike, I'm paying for the repair and I'm not sleeping with you."

"If you say so."

Had she anticipated an argument? She didn't expect him to give up so easily. But maybe he figured, wrongly, that he could change her mind. He was too charming and too good with that sexy mouth. She imagined he wouldn't disappoint in the bedroom. But her plan involved trapping him, not the other way around. Sleeping with him would give him power, and she was not going into that meeting tomorrow in a position of weakness.

"You got a helmet?" she asked, retrieving hers.

"Never wear one."

Of course he didn't. Another bad decision, she thought.

"Then let's go." She lifted her leg and slipped it neatly over the saddle, then knocked back the kickstand. Once she had the bike in Neutral and the clutch in, she rocked them forward and turned the wheel away from the line of trucks. It took a moment for gravity to grab hold, but by the time they reached the road they were gliding at five miles an hour. She shifted with her foot to second, waited until they hit fifteen miles an hour and then popped the clutch. The engine turned over and she gave it some gas. A moment later, they were ripping down the road.

"Where's your shop?"

He called directions as he slipped his hands around her waist. It felt good, riding with him. She loved the bike, despite what her mother thought, and knew that in this, at least, they would find common ground.

His body warmed her back as they raced in the direction of Koun'nde, one of three settlements here on the Turquoise Canyon Apache Indian Reservation.

After a few minutes he pointed out his place. The two-story building was mostly dark except for the floodlight over the double-bay doors. She could see a row of windows above the shop and knew that was where he lived.

She rolled up to the bay doors and cut the engine. Something moved to her left, an animal, big and black. Beth startled.

"That's just my dog, Hemi."

She glanced back at him. "Like the motor?"

His smile showed a kind of appreciation that warmed her far more than it should have. "That's right."

He slid off the bike and she removed her helmet, leaving it on the seat.

"Nice ride," he said, and then he turned to Hemi and scratched her behind the ears. "Hemi, this is Beth."

She dropped the kickstand and straddled the bike,

offering her hand to the canine, who had a definite wolfish look to her.

"Hey there, Hemi," said Beth.

Hemi took two steps in her direction and then dropped to the ground, her head between her front paws. Beth's brow wrinkled as she watched the dog, trying to interpret this odd behavior.

"What's with that?" she asked, lifting her gaze to Ty, who was now scowling at her.

"You packing?"

"What?"

"Hemi says you're carrying a gun."

Beth eyed the dog. Likely his brother would have warned her about the gunpowder-sniffing dog if she'd told anyone what she had in mind. She hadn't because the chances were too great that Jake would tip off his big brother.

Forrest had agreed, but she had only one shot, because every agent he put on the abduction case was one less on the eco-extremist investigation.

Beth set her jaw and glared at the dog.

"So what is it?" asked Ty.

She opened her jacket and showed him the holster and her service weapon. She did not show him the FBI shield she had around her neck and under her blouse.

Ty's expression went grim and all anticipation left his eyes. They went flat and lifeless. He looked at her as if she had disappointed him. That would be ironic.

"I don't allow weapons in my place."

"Girl's got a right to protect herself."

"Deal breaker," he said.

"You act like you're on parole."

That made him glare. So he didn't like being painted as a criminal, even if that was just what he was.

"Not on parole," he said, raking a hand through his hair. "Tell you what. I'll get you started again. Take it to Piñon Forks. Spend the night at the casino and call Ron in the morning." He grabbed a pen from his shop and extended his hand for hers. She gave it to him and he wrote a number on the palm of her hand.

Was he actually sending her off? Beth couldn't believe it and she really couldn't believe that her disappointment was way more physical than emotional. Damn him and that kiss.

"He's good with bikes," said Ty.

"Where's his shop?"

"Across from the police station. You know where that is, right?"

He didn't wait for her to answer, just positioned himself behind her bike. She didn't even have her helmet on when he started to push as if he could not wait to be rid of her.

But he wasn't. Not by a long shot.

Chapter Six

On Sunday mornings, Ty worked on his own projects. Today it was body repair on the 1978 Pontiac Trans Am that he'd saved from the scrap yard. But his enthusiasm for muscle cars did not generally get him up at 5:00 a.m. Still, that was what had happened the last two mornings and he knew exactly who to blame for that. The woman—Beth.

She captivated him. Not just the way she looked but the way she handled that bike and how she knew things, like that his dog was named after his favorite engine and how to bump-start a bike. Who was he kidding? It had been their kisses that had kept him from sleep.

Beth was too good to be true. Women like that did not just show up in your life. Someone had sent her. And that was the other reason he could not sleep. It wasn't the Wolf Posse. She didn't have the look of Russian mob. That left cop.

"Damn." He threw aside the rag he used to wipe his hands.

The phone rang, echoing in the empty space. He

glanced at the clock on the wall to see it was already eight in the morning. Ty reached for the greasy handset. Jake was on the line, telling him that they needed him to come into the station.

Ty's stomach dropped. Had the tribe reversed their decision about not turning him over to the Feds? As much as Ty wanted to be free of the Wolf Posse, a prison cell was not his chosen route. He had driven Kacey to the Russians, but her statement corroborated his. She had known where he was taking her and gotten into his vehicle voluntarily.

Maybe they matched his blood from the window at Antelope Lake. Some trumped-up charge on B&E? he wondered. The coffee he'd had for breakfast now clung to his stomach lining like motor oil.

"I'll be there," he said. He thought about his go-bag, the one under his bed. He'd added to it bit by bit, knowing that someday he'd have to use it.

Was today that day?

You could only dance with the devil for so long. Eventually the devil had to be paid. What kept him here was his mother and his brothers and the looming threat of his father's return.

They were all worried about what would happen upon Colton Redhorse's return. Ty wasn't worried because he knew how it would go—badly. Because people didn't change except to get worse.

He'd have to leave in forty minutes because the ride from Koun'nde to Piñon Forks took twenty. Ty removed his welding helmet and hung it back on the wall. Then he turned off the tanks. Friday, he'd spoken to tribal police and he'd made his position very clear. He didn't imagine that Detective Bear Den was going to have a second round of asking for his cooperation. So that meant they were going to charge him.

It was his own stupid fault. He must be losing his edge because he did not make that incredibly sexy woman as a cop. The way she hugged those curves on her bike, the woman could ride. And that kiss. Ty growled and headed upstairs with Hemi at his heels.

He showered and packed a duffel in case they kept him. Ty dragged out the go-bag from beneath his bed and unzipped it. Inside was survival gear, camping gear, first-aid supplies, ready-to-eat food, tools, money, a horse bridle and the keys to one car and one bike. Was today the day he'd need to run?

Ty carried both duffels to the GTO. Then he fed Hemi. After they'd both eaten, he took his dog to his mother's place. His mother, May, lived on the high ground outside Piñon Forks. Redhorse was busy getting his sister, Abbie, and the foster girls ready for church. She tried to feed him, of course, and accepted a kiss on the cheek. He asked Burt Rope, her new husband, to look after Hemi.

Burt knew exactly what that meant. "You in trouble, son?"

"Maybe. Tribal police want to talk to me again."

"Three times, isn't it?"

"Four." Four times and each time they had more pieces of the puzzle. Maybe they'd just take a blood sample today and let him go.

"We'll look after your dog, Ty." Burt laid a hand on Ty's shoulder and gave him a little pat.

Burt was a good man. Not like his rotten of a father. He felt relieved that his mother had found a man who, though not very industrious, was as reliable and kind as any he'd ever met.

Ty drove to tribal headquarters in his '67 Pontiac GTO because he didn't want to leave his bike outside the station. Burt could pick up his car. But no one drove his Harley but him.

Way he figured, tribal was done asking for his help. So they would either charge him or turn him over to the Feds. The only good thing about the attention of the police was it had kept Faras Pike from pulling him all the way back into the Wolf Posse.

Ty rolled his shoulder, wondering if Kee would be willing to take the stitches out a few days early. If the Feds took his clothing and saw him without his shirt, they might just wonder how he sliced his shoulder open and then remember the blood they'd found on the shattered picture window at the house on Antelope Lake where two women had been held.

Neither Kee nor his girlfriend, the tribe's new dispatcher, had mentioned that Ty had been there. Kee thought Ty should get some credit for helping them get away from the Russian mobsters. Ty knew that the questions as to how he knew where to find them would make him vastly less heroic and possibly culpable for some serious jail time.

Ty knew about the capture because Faras told him that Ty was on call as a driver. That meant that the

Russians had sent someone after Kee's girl and he was the backup if there was trouble. Ty had been on hand when the Russian, Yury Churkin, captured Ava Hood. The rest of the job was just shadowing them to the location where the women were being held. Faras's order to Ty to drive the Russian to safety if he ran into trouble would be enough to connect Ty to the criminal organization, and down the toilet he would go with the rest of them.

He drove to the station in Piñon Forks, which had been relocated now that the dam had been reinforced by the US Army Corps of Engineers. The state of Arizona had already begun repairs to the compromised Skeleton Cliff dam above their rez.

Ty parked at the health clinic, right next door to tribal headquarters, where the police station was housed. Kee was likely up to his eyeballs in patients, since he was now the only physician on the rez. The other, Hector Hauser, was dead and Ty could not muster a drop of regret over that. Ty wondered if they'd lock him up today or just tell him not to flee. Where would he go?

Alaska, he thought. He could follow his youngest brother, Colt, up there to a wide-open state where his reputation would not dog him. More likely he'd be relocating to a cell next to his father in the federal prison down in Phoenix.

Ty made the long walk across the formal courtyard between the buildings into tribal headquarters. Once inside, he turned toward the police station. Jake greeted him in the squad room.

"I need a lawyer?" Ty asked his little brother.

Jake did not smile or make a joke. The look he cast back was deadly serious. "Don't think that will do it."

"Am I getting arrested?" he asked, glancing toward the chief's office and making eye contact with Wallace Tinnin, who rose from behind his old battered desk and collected his aluminum crutches.

"It's one of the possibilities. Ty, I think you should cooperate."

Jake didn't understand. How could he? Jake had never been on the wrong side of anything. Yet Ty's younger brother had understood how things worked well enough to ask Ty to get Faras to report to his associates that the baby Jake wanted to adopt had died. Ty had done it and hoped Jake never learned what the favor had cost him. How would his brother feel if he knew that Ty had been pulled into service driving the Russians off the rez because of that little favor?

Tinnin clicked his way to them on his crutches. The foot, broken in the blast after the dam collapse, was in a black plastic boot.

"Thanks for coming in, Ty," said the chief. "If you'll follow me, please."

Damn, they were taking him to the interrogation room. He wondered if he still had the card with his attorney's phone number in his wallet.

They locked Ty in the room for twenty minutes. Enough time for him to consider exactly what evidence they had turned up. He'd heard that the tribe had voted to turn Kacey Doka's mother over to the Feds after she was connected to the surrogate ring.

And they voted to turn over the former tribal health clinic's administrator, Betty Mills, after she broke the conditions of her agreement for cooperation by failing to tell them that Ava Hood's cover had been blown. That nearly got Ava killed, which was no skin off his nose except that Kee was in love with her. So he'd followed Churkin and waited for Kee and Hauser. Then when the shooting started he'd busted through that plate glass window and bled all over the place.

They were probably looking at him through the one-way mirror right now. He forced his bouncing knee to stillness.

The door latch turned and in stepped Detective Jack Bear Den, one of Ty's least favorite people. Bear Den held the door for Tinnin, who thumped in on his crutches, and behind him came…

Ty sat back in his chair. He did not keep his jaw from dropping as his mouth opened like a trapdoor as she strode in—Beth. There she was, the woman on the BMW sled whose kisses rocked his world. But today her eyelids did not shimmer and the liner around her eyes was not black, but was an earth tone. She was more beautiful today, with a burgundy-colored lipstick that added to her aura of authority. She wore blue slacks, practical shoes, a blazer and a white cotton blouse. The outfit made it easy for him to see her pistol, holstered at her hip, and the FBI shield and plastic ID on a lanyard about her neck. Today she radiated a different kind of power, the kind that came with the full weight of the system. Ty had run against that system often enough to know that it didn't work. At least not for him.

FB freakin' I.

Ty closed his mouth and narrowed his eyes on her.

Beth's crazy, curly beautiful wild hair was tugged back in a scalp-hugging bun and gleamed with some kind of hair product. She stood there with a triumphant glint in her lovely pale green eyes and the hint of a wicked smile curling her wide lips. The woman had counted coup on him, defeating him with a touch of the metaphorical crooked coup stick, like the plains Apache of old. And she knew it.

Ty pressed a hand to his forehead as it sank in. Faras had seen him kissing Beth. So had Chino and Quinton and at least four other members of the Wolf Posse. Everyone in the roadhouse saw him leave with her, this two-faced woman who was on the opposite side of the law. His problems just got bigger than Antelope Lake. If the posse knew who and what she was, he was a dead man.

"Good morning, Ty," she said, taking a seat across from him and laying a file folder on the table between them. "How was your weekend?"

Chapter Seven

Ty faced the FBI field agent and realized that his dream girl had just become a nightmare. How could he be so stupid? And he was double stupid because he was staring at her mouth again while hot and cold flashes rippled over his skin. Even knowing she'd used him by making everyone in that bar think they spent the night together, she still made his senses buzz like a high-voltage electric line. But not enough to get himself killed.

"What do you want?" he asked.

He'd never pegged her as FBI. She was too sleek and sexy, with none of that stiff upright bearing or penchant for following rules. That kiss had definitely been against the rules, hadn't it? If it wasn't, it sure should have been. Memories of that kiss flashed, making his skin pucker and forming a cold knot in his stomach. He didn't like being used, and that was what she had done. Played him like a harp.

Their gazes met and locked. He expected a triumphant smile. Instead she narrowed her lovely green eyes and angled her head, studying him and waiting. For what? The explosion she expected? The tantrum of a criminal pressed against the bars of his cell?

Sorry to disappoint.

There was a power about her that still called to him and he wondered how his instincts had been so thoroughly foxed. Beth had slipped right under his radar because he'd only seen a strong, confident woman who walked on the wild side. Only Hemi had seen through her mask. His dog had smelled the gunpowder and machine oil that clung to her skin when Ty had smelled only orchids and spice.

Worse still, she'd succeeded in connecting herself to him in front of everyone in that bar. Faras would be curious about her and he'd look into her background. Ty sure hoped her cover was tight or they were both dead.

Bear Den cleared his throat. Ty didn't look at him. The tribal police detective stood to the FBI agent's left, and Tinnin moved to her right, resting his armpits on his crutches. Ty could hear him working his gum. All three blocked his path to the door that he knew was locked.

He was the only one sitting. They'd placed him in a position of weakness. But he knew the game and kept his attention on this new threat.

"I'm agent Beth Hoosay. I'm a member of the Apache tribe of Oklahoma and a field agent for the FBI assigned to a special task force here in Arizona."

"How's the sled?" he asked, feeling off balance,

but forcing himself to relax past the buzzing that was now in his ears. "Get it going?"

"Just a starter motor, loose wire. Easy fix."

No doubt because she'd been the one to loosen it to begin with, he thought.

"Your boss know the company you been keeping?" he asked. If he thought to embarrass her, he failed. Her smile widened and she looked pleased with herself.

"A better question is, do you want your boss to know the company *you've* been keeping?"

Ty shifted in his seat and then told himself to sit still.

"Okay, points for you. Counting coup? You have coup sticks up there in Oklahoma, right?"

"It's on our great seal." Beth opened the file she carried. "But that's not all I've got."

She drew out a sheet of paper, laid it on the table and turned it toward him. "This is a transcript of a conversation recorded by Agent Luke Forrest on his phone. It is from the phone of Colt Redhorse, your brother, a phone given to him by Agent Forrest. It was used by Kacey Doka to call for help during her abduction."

He knew that because he'd been the one to tell her to call the FBI. That had been one of his stupider moves. But one that did help save her life.

"The pertinent portion is right here." She stretched out her arm and pointed with one well-manicured nail. "Do you recognize this conversation?"

He glanced at the page and read:

Kacey Doka: "They aren't here yet."
Driver: "Look again."
Pause.
Driver: "Exactly."
Kacey Doka: "Where's Colt?"
Driver: "Don't know. High ground, I hope. He's
a hell of a good shot. But so are they."

TY PUSHED THE page back. They had proof he'd driven
Kacey. But he'd admitted that already and they had
both his and Kacey Doka's statements. They wouldn't
hang him on that, he hoped. But they might.

"What am I looking at?"

"Don't you know?" asked Beth.

He did not reply.

"Well, then." Agent Hoosay retrieved the page and
substituted another. "This one might interest you."
She pointed. "Blood results from the shoot-out involving your brother Dr. Kee Redhorse at Antelope
Lake five days ago. Somehow Dr. Redhorse managed
to get two kidnap victims out of that house past two
armed men, yet he was unarmed and both captors had
handguns. This blood was found in the living room
on broken glass. On the dock behind the house. On
the boat that your brother used to escape and on the
shore at the northeastern shore of the lake."

Ty did not look at the page. He preferred looking
at Beth. She was so sure she had him boxed. Did she

remember that a trapped animal is the most danger-ous kind?

"It's your blood. We don't need a sample because we obtained one with a warrant from your clinic. Perfect match. So we don't need your brother Kee or Louisa Tah or former detective Ava Hood to verify your presence at Antelope Lake."

Ty propped an elbow on the table and splayed his hand over his jaw, studying her. He'd known she was beautiful at first sight. Her entrance at the roadhouse showed she had a confidence bordering on reckless-ness. She also knew how to ride a motorcycle, a beauty of a bike. He added smarts to her list of attri-butes and wondered what she'd do if he put his hand over the one beside the damning evidence.

He wouldn't, of course. They were adversaries from now on and he'd do well to remember it in-stead of noticing the way her eyes bordered on gray under the fluorescent lights.

Bear Den spoke up. "You assisted Dr. Redhorse in rescuing Ava Hood and Louisa Tah."

"You here to give me my medal?"

Bear Den's smile showed how much he was en-joying this. Ty had been a burr under Bear Den's saddle for years.

"You were there and that is no crime. But how you knew where to find your brother and Dr. Hauser might be," said Beth, the threat veiled in her soft, honeyed voice.

"Yet I'm not under arrest," he said.

The FBI agent glanced to Tinnin. "Because you

encouraged Kacey to call for backup and stayed to help her escape and you came to your brother Kee's aid on Antelope Lake. Other circumstances, you'd be a hero, son."

Ty made a face and sat back in his chair. "My whole life has been other circumstances."

"Distinguished yourself in the US Marines," added Tinnin.

"After accepting a deal to serve in lieu of facing charges for armed robbery at eighteen," Bear Den said.

Jeez. Did the detective have his file memorized?

Tinnin ignored Bear Den's comment. "We know you've helped your brothers. We want you to help your tribe the same way."

"How exactly do you expect me to do that?"

"First off, if you have any information on any criminal activity on this rez, you need to tell us now."

Ty thought of the meth lab operating on Deer Kill Meadow and kept his mouth shut.

"Nothing?" said Bear Den.

"You didn't call me in here to be a snitch. Tell me what you really want."

They told him and he laughed. "So. Take the deal or my tribe will turn me over to face federal charges. Question is, how likely is it that this deal of yours is going to get me killed?"

Agent Hoosay sat back, draping an arm over the back of her chair. Now there was the woman he had met the other night, all danger and promise.

"Now, I figured you for a risk-taker, Ty. I'm willing to take a chance on you if you're willing to give us certain assurances."

"Be your trained monkey, you mean."

Her voice was almost a purr. "I prefer to think of you as a lapdog. *My* lapdog."

"The posse has tribal police outmanned and out-gunned. And I know they drive better cars because I fix them. Plus they currently have very powerful friends."

"Victor Vitoli, Leonard Usov and the Kuznetsov crime organization."

"Ding, ding. Someone has been doing her home-work."

"We aim to break up the posse for good, son," said Tinnin. "And see that the Russian mob finds it too hot to continue operations up here."

Bear Den leaned in. "And we want the four re-maining missing girls back."

Ty wanted that, too. But it was on the list of im-possible things, like wanting to stay out of the gang or be invited to join Tribal Thunder, the warrior sect of the tribe's medicine society. He'd thought he'd put that one to bed years ago, but here it was, popping up in his mind like burned toast. He added the even more far-fetched possibility of recovering his smashed and ruined reputation to the list. Impossible. Yeah. Sometimes you were just doomed to be disappointed.

"What's the deal?" asked Ty.

"Your full cooperation in our investigation," said Beth. "And in exchange we forgo pursuit of you in connection with our investigation."

Ty nodded. "What do you expect me to do, exactly?"

"Introduce me to the Wolf Posse as your new girlfriend and give me your continued efforts to get me on the inside."

"No way." Was she crazy? Did she even know what she'd have to do to join the posse?

Bear Den smiled. Ty could see the pleasure he got in just imagining turning Ty over for federal prosecution.

"I need to get on the inside," said Beth.

"Not by joining the posse, you don't."

Tinnin interjected then. "What about just having you pose as Ty's girlfriend? That will get you into the roadhouse and access to members of the posse."

Beth rolled her lips between her teeth and drummed her fingers. She didn't seem like the kind of gal who would compromise.

"We'll start with that," she said. Her eyes offered both challenge and promise. "So, Mr. Redhorse. Do you accept this arrangement?"

Ty wondered just how realistic she wanted their relationship to be. Anticipation made his heart race. Attraction to this Fed was the most stupid reason of all to take the deal. "I accept."

Chapter Eight

It was not until he breathed fresh air that Ty had a chance to wonder whether he had accepted their deal to prevent federal prosecution, or because accepting was the only way to get near Beth. He hoped it wasn't the latter, because he liked to believe he was smarter than that.

He spotted a vehicle as he drove out of the parking lot by the tribe's headquarters with FBI agent Beth Hoosay. His eyes narrowed at the familiar black RAM pickup with the pencil-thin gold detailing. It was a truck with which he was acquainted because he'd had to do the detailing twice. Chino Aria hadn't liked the first gold Ty used because he wanted the paint to sparkle. Pain in the ass, that was what he was. Chino was also dangerous, especially to women.

Ty could think of only one reason that Chino would park his truck across the street from the police station and not be in it. The Feds had themselves another snitch. What did they have on Chino? Ty didn't know but knew that the man was one of Faras's enforcers. Ty's list of sins was black, but Chino's was blacker, as he inflicted pain and enjoyed it.

"Hedging your bets?" he asked.

"What?" asked the agent.

"If I can figure it out, so can Faras. Chino is a nitwit, a dangerous one. Parking over there, at the diner, it's a bad move. Any of the gang could see his truck."

"Chino wasn't driving it," said Beth.

Ty frowned. Who would dare drive Chino's truck? he wondered. Faras was the only answer he could come up with, but he would never come into the station. Faras was deadly and suspicious, but he would never cooperate with the police. Ty was certain.

"Who, then?" Ty asked.

Beth ignored the question.

"You don't have to worry about being spotted. Tinnin assigned an officer to watch for any of the known vehicles," said Beth. "Besides, you parked at the clinic. Very smart."

She knew where he parked his GTO. He didn't like that.

"Where my brother Kee works," said Ty.

"Your younger brother, Jake, works at for the tribal police. It gives you a reason to park in their lot."

"That's one of the things Faras likes about me— my family connections." He didn't say the rest, that Faras was a master at using those connections to keep Ty in line. "So, where to?"

"Your place. I'm moving in."

Ty smiled and gave her the kind of predatory look that made most women adjust their clothing to cover up. Beth met his stare with one of her own, cold and dangerous. The woman gave him the chills in all the right and wrong places and both at the same time.

"I don't think Hemi will like having another female around the place."

"She'll get used to me. I'm good with animals."

"Ought to make things easier on us both, then," he said.

She laughed and then glanced out the window. The music of her mirth made him want to hear it again.

"You grow up on the rez up there in Oklahoma?" he asked.

"No. I'm just on the tribal rolls. My mother's a member, so I'm entitled to membership, too." She pressed her lips together and her eyes shifted and narrowed. What was making her angry? A memory of the tribe, her mother? Ty's instincts said there was something back there that nettled.

"They have a blood requirement?"

She shot him a glance that seemed laced with poison. Was it because his question implied she would not meet most tribal requirements? If so, perhaps he had just found a chink in her armor.

"The requirement is one sixteenth Oklahoma Apache unless you have a parent enrolled. I meet either prerequisite."

Yup, she was prickly as a cholla cactus and all signs of humor had fled from her features.

"I've never lived anywhere but here," said Ty.

"You've been out there, though. US Marines."

She could read, he thought, and realized that she

also would know why he joined. Some of the reasons anyway. Now he was frowning, too. Back then, he had tried going to the police. But his mother would not press charges and he was too young to do it. All he'd managed was to get protective services out to their place, which scared Jake and Colt so much he'd never done it again. He didn't want his father hitting his mother, but he also didn't want his brothers separated through the foster-care system. Jake had called soon afterward, though, still believing in the system that had let them down. That had been one particularly bad night after Ty had tried and failed to defeat his father. It had been satisfying seeing his father loaded into Tinnin's patrol car. But he'd been out in less than twenty-four hours. Ty had learned an important lesson that day. He'd learned that bones took longer to heal than it took to get out of jail after assaulting your wife.

Beth spoke again, prompting confirmation. "Distinguished yourself in Iraq. Isn't that right?"

"Yeah, I was a jarhead," said Ty. Back then he'd considered reenlistment. But he couldn't because his family needed him here. Ty had come back home when Colt received his psych discharge.

"Ever think of leaving the rez?" she asked.

"Sometimes."

She cast him a puzzled look. Had she ever felt trapped?

"Why the FBI?" he asked as they left the main community and the river behind and headed toward Koun'nde.

"Oh, well, I'll give you the official version first." She cleared her throat and raised her chin a notch. "Growing up in Oklahoma after the bombing that put us on the map, I felt a need to protect our nation from threats both domestic and foreign."

Now he was even more curious. Was she really trying to save the world? Her smile seemed to challenge, as if asking if he swallowed that tale.

"The unofficial version?" he asked.

She faced forward again, gazing out the windshield as they passed the river and the ongoing reconstruction of the destroyed dam.

No answer, he thought, was still an answer. What part of her past dogged her?

"I have to stop and get my dog."

"At your mother's?"

She knew his mother. Likely knew more about him than he did. He didn't like it, the advantage she had over him. He wondered if Jake could find out anything about her with his databases. Did his brother have anyone up there in Oklahoma who he could ask for information on Beth? But the Oklahoma Apache tribe was not like this rez. The tribe was huge and a conglomeration of many Apache people. Oklahoma City was huge as well. If Ty was going to learn anything about his opponent, he'd have to get the information from the source.

Ty never liked handling explosives, and Beth seemed more dangerous than the IEDs back in the sandbox. If she blew their cover, he'd be dead. If she blew the arrest, he'd be dead. That didn't scare him as much as knowing that when a bomb detonates, it was indiscriminate with collateral damage. Jake and Kee were here, in close range. His mother and her new husband and his little sister, Abbie, were all so very close. And each one was a weapon to use against him. He'd stayed as long as his presence served to keep them safe. When that changed, he'd take off.

Ty adjusted his hands on the wheel and stepped on the gas. In a few minutes, they arrived at his mother's place. Burt Rope was out in the yard watering down the dusty driveway and greeted them with a wave.

"Well, what a nice surprise. You missed Sunday supper," said Burt.

The largest meal of the week was served at noon, after church. His brothers Jake and Kee were now bringing their significant others. Ty was almost happy he'd been in the interrogation room, because the idea of joining his family for the Sunday meal with this woman posing as his girlfriend did not sit well.

They were all gone, thank goodness. He knew this because their trucks weren't there.

He asked in any case. "They gone?"

"Yup. Jake took the girls, too. Off to visit their younger brothers," said Burt.

Jeffery and Hewett were fostering with one of the tribal council members, Hazel Tran, because Ty's mother just couldn't house two more children.

"Abbie, too?" he asked, getting out of the car.

"Abbie, too." Burt turned to Beth, who now stood on the drive beside the passenger side of the GTO. "Who's this?"

Ty made introductions. Beth shook hands. Neither her weapon nor her shield was in evidence and she seemed as if she'd just come from church, instead of his funeral.

"I didn't know that Ty had sisters," said Beth.

Like hell, he thought. She thought she knew everything about him. But that was impossible.

"Oh, he has one, plus three more now. We've taken them in."

The Doka girls included sixteen-year-old Jackie, thirteen-year-old Winnie and eleven-year-old Shirley. Three girls, four including his sister, and all the right age for the Russians to pluck like flowers. Ty knew that his cooperation was what kept them from entering the rolls of removal. Faras had said as much and as head of the Wolf Posse, he made the selections. But now, with the doctor killed at Antelope Lake, operations had ceased. For now. He feared that this was a temporary respite.

And the FBI was so concerned about their problems that they had allocated one single agent. Now he must decide if he would add her to his growing list of those he must protect, or throw her to the wolves.

BETH ENJOYED MEETING his mother and Burt Rope. She knew all about them on paper, but she appreciated meeting the real version. His mother's life had been difficult. She'd married young to a violent man who had been in and out of jail until the felonies piled high enough to make him serve real time. Despite that, May Redhorse had managed to get all four of her boys raised and each had graduated from high school. Two had additional higher education. May had a big heart, obviously, because she was fostering the Doka girls, though she had neither the room nor the resources to do so. The girls were lucky. They would likely have a chance now, Beth decided, all because of May.

Ty introduced Beth as his girlfriend, as arranged. Beth felt a twinge of guilt at the joy on May's face. Did his mother see the promise of grandchildren when she looked at Beth? Beth had been undercover for up to six months at a time. But somehow fooling this woman made her feel dirty.

She was relieved when they finally left, having been fed lunch, of course, from the leftovers of the Sunday supper they had missed.

The stop to pick up his dog had lasted over an hour. Hemi now sat in the rear seat, her eyes half-closed and her tongue lolling.

"She's a great cook," said Beth as they returned to the car. "And quite a woman."

"Yes."

"She's strong like her sons."

But not her body, thought Beth. Her body was dying bit by bit because of the diabetes and the diet she had not altered. Fry bread and sugary baked goods were abundant in the house.

"I don't want you to see her again," Ty said.

"Why?"

"Because I don't bring my women here. Coming here makes you special to her. I don't want you to be special."

He was right, of course. So she couldn't understand why it hurt her that he wanted distance between her and his mom. Under other circumstances, they might have been friends.

"It's good that you look out for her," she said.

He snorted but said nothing.

"Lucky she didn't lose you and your dad both after that robbery."

Ty's laugh held little humor. "Yeah. Lucky."

"Your age, I mean. Protecting you."

"You could see it that way."

Now he had her attention. "How do you see it?"

"Hey, I'm just glad he's gone."

"But he's up for parole again."

His grim expression showed that he knew that all too well. Ty pulled into the drive in front of his shop in the golden light of late afternoon. The landscape was lovely here and changed by the mile. The river rushed along beside the road in places and there were vistas of rocky bluffs and mountains. She had yet to see the ridges of turquoise from which the tribe derived its name. The territory was so different than the city where she lived and the flat plains that surrounded it. Hemi stood in the backseat and stretched. Ty let her out first, leaving Beth to collect her gear and follow them into his place.

"Apartment is up that way." Ty pointed to the stairs that ran up the outside of the building. "It's unlocked."

He left her, returning to his shop and the rusty Ford Impala in the second bay.

She settled into the upstairs apartment that Ty

called home, dropping her bag beside the couch before going to explore. The main area was divided into a tiled kitchen-dining combo and a carpeted living room. Anchored to one wall was a long couch, draped in a brightly colored Navajo blanket. Above the couch was a framed vintage poster of a Model 101 Indian motorcycle.

She smiled. "Can't argue with that."

That bike was a classic.

In front of the couch, there was a square maple coffee table with a stack of *Popular Mechanics* magazines on it, along with the motorcycle auction news. Between the table and kitchen, a worn leather recliner faced a modest-size flat-screen TV. Before the television was a large padded circular dog bed, the faux-sheepskin inner lining liberally sprinkled with dark hair.

A window flanked one side of the television. Bookshelves lined the other side. He had a good collection of mysteries and thrillers, plus some biographies. But most of the shelving was filled with framed photographs.

His brothers at all stages of life grinned at her. His sister as a toddler, on Ty's skinny knee. His mother in full regalia. Kee in a cast sitting in a hospital bed surrounded by his family. There was one person noticeable in his absence from Ty's collection. He had no photos of his father, Colton Redhorse, on display.

The only actual photo Beth owned was in her wallet. It was of her mom and dad and her, back when they were happy and whole. The rest of her photographic memories of her family were at her mother's home in boxes.

The remainder of the upstairs consisted of a short hallway. On one side was a full bathroom with white porcelain tub, sink and toilet and a small study. On the other side of the hall sat the master bedroom with a queen-sized bed, reading chair and bureau. The bed was also covered in a Navajo-style wool blanket, this one in red, black and yellow.

She had not expected his inner sanctum to be so scrupulously clean and Spartan. He lived like a man in a monastery. All the flash of his bike and the style and character of the cars he restored did not transfer to his apartment.

Beth headed to Ty's bedroom and poked around. His clothing was also utilitarian. Jeans, not too tight or loose. Worn, but not worn out. T-shirts in muted colors. She found no jewelry, no rings or necklaces, no earrings or hair adornments. He liked leather for his jackets, boots and belts. She found no drugs or weapons of any sort. Why didn't he carry a weapon?

She wondered how Ty had survived so long without one or if, perhaps, his unwillingness to carry a weapon had kept him alive. She liked a puzzle, and Ty was that. In spades.

There was nothing of interest under his bed but a stuffed squeaky toy squirrel that she guessed, from the teeth marks, belonged to Hemi. Beside that was an old baseball glove cupped around a tennis ball. In his bedside table he had batteries, a lighter, a candle in a glass jar. She sniffed, inhaling the scent of balsa wood and pine. The drawer also held a flashlight and condoms.

Her search of his bureau and bathroom turned up no drugs, legal or otherwise except for extra strength BC Powder. Ty did not take drugs, apparently, and suffered from no more than an occasional headache. Meanwhile she carried a roll of antacid tablets perpetually in her pocket and chewed them like breath mints. The acidic condition of her belly being a result of stress, according to her doctor.

"What gives you headaches, Ty?" she asked her reflection in the medicine cabinet. "Your family? The gang? The police? Your conscience?"

Beth returned the packets to their place.

Where were the clues to a man whom she had not yet placed in his proper box? Chief Tinnin believed Ty was a tragic hero. Bear Den believed he was a criminal who had slipped from the noose.

Who was right?

As it got later in the afternoon, Beth joined Ty in his garage, hoping she would gain more insights from him there.

He lifted his head at her arrival.

"Find anything interesting?" he asked.

"Nice selection of condoms," she said, hoping to wipe that smug smile from his mouth.

"I aim to please," he replied, and returned to his work.

Now she was the one blushing. She perched on a stool beside his workbench with her laptop on a clean rag spread upon the surface. Hemi appeared from beyond the bay doors and settled into her dog bed at Beth's feet. She stared at the dog, who regarded her with one open eye. It was a neat trick, spotting weapons. She wondered if it was the scent of gunpowder or the gun oil that alerted the canine. And she wondered if Hemi knew any more tricks.

Tonight Ty would be introducing her as his new woman at the bar. She had been right to meet him there first. It gave her a much-needed advantage and the leverage necessary to gain his help.

At 5:00 p.m., Ty finished work and used some goop to clean the grease off his forearms and hands. The process was a sensual glide of skin on skin. Beth tried not to be mesmerized, but failed. She liked tattoos and appreciated the US Marine Corps insignia on his arm. It was, unfortunately, beneath the one near his elbow that marked him as a member of the tribe's gang.

Upstairs Ty left her to shower. Beth dressed in her costume and carefully applied the makeup that said she was trouble. She liked this mask. It gave her a different kind of power and the edge she needed to take on the role. The best kind of power came from military rank and now her FBI shield. She still had both, but now she also had red lipstick. She let down her hair and worked in the product until it coiled in wild ringlets. Then she popped an antacid as a preemptive strike against nerves.

Ty appeared in black jeans, a white T-shirt and a brown bomber jacket that looked vintage. His feet were covered with motorcycle boots, of course, and he radiated danger. Nearly irresistible, she thought.

What he didn't wear were gang colors. Ty somehow operated on the gang's periphery, and she didn't understand why.

On the drive to the roadhouse, she tried and failed to ignore the spicy scent of his aftershave. He spoke first.

"You work gangs before?"

"No."

"No gangs?" He was frowning now, as if he had already decided she was not the woman for the job.

"It won't be a problem. I've been briefed by our experts."

"Any of those experts actually been in a gang?" Ty asked.

"No. Of course not."

"If you have no experience with gangs, Agent Hoosay, why are you here?"

"You should start calling me Beth."

"Sure."

"I was asked to join the task force because I have specialized knowledge regarding organized crime."

"And because you're Apache," he said, his words accusatory.

She did not quite keep herself from making a face. "It's not a factor."

He actually laughed. "You think they could have sent a male agent to do what you're about to do?"

She didn't.

"They picked you because you're hot, young, enrolled in an Apache tribe and stupid enough, or hungry enough, to take some monster risks. What is it you're after, exactly? Promotion? Accolades? Make Mama proud?"

She pressed her lips together and watched him. Finally she gave him something. "I wanted out of Oklahoma City."

"You have a bike. Easy to get out."

"Is it? So why are you still here?"

"Touché," he said.

She turned to watch him as she spoke, his strong jaw illuminated by the dashboard light. He certainly was easy on the eyes.

"I was stationed in DC. Worked at Quantico and I got interested in the FBI."

"Stationed?"

"US Army."

Ty groaned.

She ignored it. "I applied to the Bureau and they took me."

"And assigned you back to Oklahoma?" he asked, guessing correctly.

"Exactly. Plunked me right back where I started because I was familiar with the territory."

"Ironic. And reassignment to a bigger field office requires you to make a case—a big one. Isn't that right?"

Now, how did he know that? She was constantly reassessing him and still she'd underestimated him again.

"What you work on up there?"

"Organized crime for the last five years. I know this group. We know every player."

"Yet they're still walking around."

"Hopefully, you can help change that."

"I'm just going to get you proximity. That was the deal I signed."

Beth smiled, but said nothing to reassure him.

"You don't want them gone?" she asked.

"Depends on the cost." He changed the subject. "Why do you want out of Oklahoma?"

She snorted. No way was she answering that. "The Midwest is too flat."

"What about Arizona?"

"It's not flat."

"Is that what you're leaving behind?" he asked. "The landscape?"

She didn't answer. His questions had turned too personal. "You have my cover story down?"

"Yes, ma'am."

He pulled into the lot, already half-full with a variety of pickups and bikes. It did not escape her that most of the vehicles were some variety of the gang's colors, black and gold.

Ty cut the engine of the GTO, and the world went quiet for just a moment before the sounds of music from within the roadhouse reached her. Beth's heartbeat pulsed and her skin prickled a warning as she faced the lion's den with only Ty Redhorse as her backup.

He grinned. "Ready to meet my friends?"

Chapter Nine

Ty tried not to admire the way that Beth had dressed
for success in tight blue jeans and a hip-length brown
suede jacket that tied at the waist and hid the pistol
she now had in the inner pocket. The jacket gaped
open to show a tight V-necked top in cherry-red that
revealed enough cleavage to make a man want more
and to take his attention away from her face. The red
matched the color of her lipstick. Ty loved a woman in
high boots, and hers were high and laced up the front.

Inside the bar the Sunday football game still blared
on the television and patrons at the bar cheered as the
Houston Texans' kicker sent the ball through the up-
rights for a field goal.

Ty kept an arm about her as they entered, staking
a claim. But at the bar, Beth chatted up several of the
customers, zeroing in on any wearing gold and black.
Ty beat her at pool because she let him and they drew
a crowd. Faras claimed winner, but he didn't want to
play Ty, so he stepped aside and let Beth do her job.

She was good. Just the right amount of charm and
allure. Not overdone, but when Faras invited her to

the Wolf Den, Ty stepped in and told them the two of them had plans. He cast Beth a warning look that you would have to be blind not to see.

She ignored it. Was he responsible for her safety if she did stupid things that might get her seriously messed up? He growled as he realized that, even if she deserved it, he could not let her go to the Wolf Den alone.

He was prepared to advise her on what a bad idea going into their crib could be for a woman, but she turned down the invitation, looping her arm in Ty's as she chatted with Faras.

Ty scanned the occupants of the bar. There were the usual characters and a large number of the posse, who were watching the game on the large-screen television. Eight men plus the one outside. Just the ones he could see outnumbered the tribal police force by two, and there were more, Ty knew. Five women, all longtime members of the posse, watched Beth from their usual table. None were exclusive except for Jewell. She'd risen in the ranks to become a favorite with Faras. Ty knew why. Jewell was young, only twenty, but she was cunning and beautiful, the female version of an alpha.

The last true couple in the Wolf Posse had been Minnie and Trey. But Trey got clipped and Minnie switched horses, going with Earle. Now they were both awaiting trial. Ty smiled as he thought of his small part in their capture. Hemi had done most of it. Luckily, Hemi wasn't talking and the FBI kept anyone from seeing those two so they had no chance to spill the beans to Faras that Ty had been there watching over Jake and his new baby girl.

He saw Jewell speaking to Chino and sensed trouble. Faras was paying too much attention to Beth for Jewell to do nothing, and Ty's claim on Beth meant nothing because all here knew that Faras took what and whom he wanted.

Jewell ambled over and took Ty's other arm, giving Chino the chance he needed to drag Beth from his side. Jewell clung tight as Chino propositioned Beth.

"Maybe you'd like to stay up here on Turquoise Canyon. Join our group," said Chino, drawing Beth before him and moving in way too close.

Beth shifted away and Chino tugged her back. Ty realized she was trying to prevent him from feeling the gun in her jacket pocket.

Uh-oh, Ty thought, unfolding his arms as he reached the coffee table and Beth, trapped between Faras and Chino. Time to go.

Beth was FBI, but she'd worked organized crime. Did she know what was involved with a woman joining a gang?

"Just a small initiation," said Chino, unable to keep the smile of anticipation from curling his lips.

"No," said Ty, extracting himself from Jewell's ferocious grip. Her job done, Jewell moved beside Faras.

Chino kept a hold on Beth and faced Ty. "Why not let the lady decide?"

Ty looked to Faras to settle the argument. He didn't. Instead, he lifted his hands from his beer bottle and offered them palms up.

"Settle it outside," said Faras.

Chino rose to his feet and bumped Ty with his shoulder on the way past. Ty grabbed Beth and muscled her toward the rear exit.

"What are you doing?" she asked.

"Getting you out of here."

"I'm not going without you," she said.

"Only way out for me is through Chino," he said.

Ty watched the big man head through the door, followed by several of the men and all the women.

"Don't go out there," said Beth.

"You want to be my girl? This is how it's done. If you plan to hang on the posse's turf, I have to establish my singular claim."

"That's barbaric."

"So are they."

Beth hesitated, looking toward the back of the roadhouse.

"We won't make it," said Ty.

"Well, I can't let him kill you."

Ty nodded. Beth had assessed their chances, pictured the encounter and decided Ty would not only lose, but also be killed. Her confidence was touching.

"If I help you, I have to blow my cover."

"Who asked you to help me?" said Ty, and headed for the door.

She grabbed him before he went outside. There

in the entrance, between the roadhouse and the lot, he faced her.

"Do you know what the initiation involves?" His words came as a rasp, like a file on metal.

She looked at the dirty rug advertising Coors beer. Her words where flat, as if she was just reciting them. "Crime is a standard initiation for males. For a female, it's sex."

She lifted her gaze and their eyes met.

"Exactly." Ty wiped his face with both hands. "I don't like you, Agent Hoosay, but I'll protect you if I can."

Now he saw the worry in her eyes, and her hand went into her jacket pocket, reaching for the pistol he knew was secreted there.

He grabbed her wrist and pulled her close, speaking against her temple. "No."

She clung to his shirt with her free hand. "It's a last resort."

"You can run, but you cannot draw that pistol. If you do, I'm a dead man because I brought you here. Do you understand?"

"But what if—"

"Do you understand?" he growled.

"Yes." Her voice was breathless.

"While I'm fighting, you're backing up until you get to my car and then you are out of here." He held up the key fob.

She took it.

Ty pressed his lips to the top of her head and closed his eyes.

"You don't have to do this," she said again.

"Either you're mine or you're not. No middle ground."

Then he let her go and stepped out to the lot, where the circle of spectators waited. There in the center stood Chino.

"Thought you snuck out the back," said Chino.

"Had to take a piss," he said.

"When I'm done with you, you'll piss yourself again," snarled Chino.

Several in the gathering laughed at this.

The man looked positively delighted, though whether at the prospect of fighting Ty or sleeping with Beth, Ty did not know.

Faras arrived behind Ty with Quinton at his side.

"Come on!" Chino was already flexing and snorting like a bull preparing to charge.

Ty looked to Faras, who sighed. Then he gave Ty a slow shake of his head.

"She worth it?" asked Faras.

Ty did not hesitate and nodded once.

"Then you got to prove it."

"You won't blame me if I damage your man," he said, thumbing toward Chino.

That caused many of the watching Wolf Posse members to laugh out loud. Faras didn't laugh because Faras had seen Ty fight.

Chino roared and charged without waiting for Faras to answer the question.

He came at Ty with his shoulders back and chest out. Most fights started with shoving and jostling, sometimes with a chest or belly bump. Ty never wasted time or effort with posturing. Chino was bigger. But he wouldn't win.

Ty glanced to Beth. She wasn't backing up. Worse still, she clearly thought Chino would win, because she had her hand in her jacket pocket again.

Chapter Ten

Beth wrapped her hand around her service pistol and used one finger to flick off the safety while keeping her eyes on Ty and Chino.

She'd been undercover before and thought she knew what she was doing, but somehow in less than twelve hours she had managed to put both herself and her contact in jeopardy.

Chino lifted a hand to shove Ty. It was a sloppy first move.

His hand never made contact. Ty grasped his wrist and spun him so fast the entire thing was a blur. Chino folded at the waist as Ty forced his wrist up behind his back, using only his thumb as leverage. Then Ty ran him across the circle. The members in the gathering marked Chino's course and moved aside a moment before Chino's head hit the door of the pickup parked in the handicapped spot. The car door was dented on impact.

Ty let him go, which Beth thought was an incredibly stupid thing to do.

Chino rose from the ground, roaring as he turned like a Kodiak bear preparing to charge.

Ty looked to Faras and lifted his hands as if asking for directions or perhaps hoping Faras would call this off. Faras nodded his consent and Ty's shoulders sank and he turned his attention back to Chino. Beth thought Faras had just given Ty the okay to continue. Ty would have to finish this fight. But what were the rules? Did they fight until someone conceded, or what?

Ty rolled his shoulder. Chino fixed on the movement, sensing weakness like a shark senses blood.

Speaking of which, was that blood on the front of Ty's T-shirt? His bomber jacket was unzipped and the shirt beneath glistened in a way she associated with blood. Beth knew that Ty had been injured at Antelope Lake and that he had lost a significant amount of blood because of the samples collected. She'd seen the photos, but she did not know where exactly Ty had been injured while crashing through the picture window. She also could not get her mind around how a man with that much blood loss could manage to make it twenty-three miles over rough ground back to his rez, on foot and alone.

Chino's eyes narrowed as he shook out his arm and rubbed his sore thumb. She knew Chino had an eighth-grade education, had been expelled for bringing a weapon to his middle school and had been arrested twice for shoplifting and drug possession. Meanwhile, Ty Redhorse had served in the US Marine Corps. Had distinguished himself in several

combat engagements and had left with an honorable discharge.

Size aside, she now had her money on the warrior.
Quinton wandered over to stand beside her.

Beth rested her free hand on her hip as her sweaty
hand gripped the pistol. Quinton folded his arms and
leaned against the truck bed behind them as Chino
took his first swing.

"Wish I had the guts to challenge Chino sometimes, but he'd break me in two pieces like a dry
stick," said Quinton, and then pantomimed the break.
"Snap!"

Beth cut her gaze away from Quinton and back
to the fight.

"I'm Quinton."

She knew who he was. Quinton had finished high
school. Barely. He'd been in the tribe's jail for three
months after a bar fight that tribal suspected was
gang-related. He'd lost the fight, which was how the
police picked him up, bleeding all over himself.

"Beth," she said, and was forced to release her pistol to shake his hand.

"This has been coming for a while. Chino hates
Ty."

"Why's that?"

Beth hoped she would not have to draw her weapon
to keep one male from killing the other. She did not
want to blow her cover, but she was not going to
watch this gorilla kill Ty. Especially when Ty was
defending her.

"Chino resents that Ty gets to come and go as

he likes. That Faras shows him a kind of respect he doesn't give the rest of us. But those two got a long history. Back to high school. Almost like Faras owes Ty or something."

Chino's second swing was clumsy and Ty ducked under it.

"Brewing for a while is all." Quinton motioned to the women, all sitting on the open gate of a pickup across the circle, glaring daggers at her. "Looks like you haven't made any friends here yet but Faras."

Ty glided under Chino's flailing arm, punched him in the kidney and watched the big man sink to his knees.

"Down goes Frazier," said Quinton, imitating Howard Cosell's famous words. "You a fight fan?"

"No."

"Got a favorite?" asked Quinton.

"I like the horse I rode in on."

Ty cast her a look and motioned his head toward his car. He'd given her plenty of time to escape. But she wasn't leaving him here wrestling that gorilla.

"I'd love to see Chino land just one punch," said Quinton.

"Why's that?"

Quinton shrugged. "Pretty boy. Teacher's pet."

It seemed Ty did not have many friends among the gang, either, except perhaps Faras Pike himself.

Chino started to rise and Ty kicked him in the head with his booted foot. Chino fell facedown, hard. Ty was on Chino's back an instant later. Ty had the man's beefy arm up over his head and bent his arm back toward his shoulder blade until his wrist nearly met his shoulder.

Chino cried out and kicked.

Beth took a step forward. Ty increased the pressure on Chino's shoulder, and the man stopped struggling.

Ty had won and chosen to spare Chino's life, which was great because it kept Beth from having to arrest him for manslaughter.

"Yield," demanded Ty.

Chino's eyes were bloodshot and his mouth screwed up like that of a man who ate limes for a living. Finally he nodded.

"Yield," Chino said.

Ty rose and his opponent rolled to his back. Ty offered his hand. Chino hesitated, then looked at Faras, who inclined his chin by the slightest measure. Chino snorted but accepted Ty's help to his feet.

Beth slipped her hand from her jacket and glanced to Faras, who pinned her with a steady stare. Did he suspect she had a weapon or, worse, did he suspect who and what she was?

Ty remained where he was as Chino shuffled back toward Faras; then he turned to Beth.

"You're still here," he said through clenched teeth.

"Didn't want to miss your win."

"Win? All I did was make Chino even more determined to kill me."

She looped her arm in the crook of his elbow, casting a glance around at the crowd, who would all watch Ty Redhorse leave with her.

"You are both welcome at the crib anytime," Faras called after them.

Beth lifted her hands and wiggled her fingers in farewell. Ty's breathing was heavy and his face was pale. She glanced at his shoulder. His black T-shirt was definitely wet and she suspected it was wet with blood. His blood. She needed to get him home and find out what was wrong with him.

She lifted the keys. "I'll drive."

"Thank God," he said.

"Hospital?"

"No."

Beth clenched her jaw and didn't argue, ignoring the flutter of worry in her chest. He was a contact. Not her man. Though he had just fought as if he was. It was a level of commitment you couldn't get with threats or bribes. She knew that, but she didn't want to think about it or what it meant.

She did admit, to herself at least, that Ty was not what she had expected.

"Did you know that might happen when you agreed to this?" she asked.

"I knew it was likely."

"How?"

"Because Chino has challenged me before. Any excuse."

"Has he ever bested you?"

"No. But sooner or later he's going to stop playing fair."

She'd put him in danger and he'd fought to protect her. It required acknowledgment.

"Thank you for getting him off me," she said.

He turned to stare for a long moment. Then he said, "Bet that wasn't easy to say."

That made her smile. "You're not what I expected, Ty."

He turned back to look out the window. His words seemed spoken more to himself. "That's because no one expects much."

Beth got him back to his place. She walked behind him as they mounted the outside steps, keeping one hand on his lower back. She ignored the flexing of the strong muscles that rippled beneath the thin fabric of his shirt and concentrated on supporting him. Ty unlocked the door. Hemi charged at them and then skidded to a halt, her toenails scraping on the tile floor. Then she dropped to the ground and whined.

"I know she's got a gun, Hemi." Ty extended his hand and Hemi rose, still whining. His dog knew something was wrong. Ty motioned her outside, but she wouldn't go. Beth admired the canine's loyalty. Hemi was staying right where she was until she knew that her master was all right.

Beth drew out a kitchen chair.

"Sit," said Beth to Ty. He did. Hemi did not.

She removed her jacket and slipped her pistol into the waistband of her jeans, in the center of her back. Then she got his jacket off. The sticky black T-shirt left a smear of blood when she dragged it up and over his head. Now Beth saw what Hemi smelled. Blood coated the strong muscles of his chest and torso, painting them crimson. Across the top of one shoulder was the cause of the torrent. A six-inch wound cut a jagged course across his flesh. Someone with skill had sutured the laceration, his oldest brother, she suspected, but a one-inch section had torn open.

"Call Kee," said Ty. Then he closed his eyes.

"Do you feel sick?"

"Tired. Tired of fighting and lying and…" His words fell off.

"Is this wound from Antelope Lake?" she asked.

Someone had helped Kee overpower Yury Churkin, the Russian crime family's hired assassin, and taken on the other man on guard in the house. Kee had managed to get to two missing women with the help of his mentor, Hector Hauser, who turned out to be up to his eyeballs in the entire mess. Both captives were rescued, Kee escaped, Hauser was shot and killed along with one of the Russian guards. Yury Churkin had shot himself to avoid arrest. And Ty had been there. The blood evidence said so.

Beth wadded his shirt and used it as a compression bandage, pressing it tight to the wound.

Beth suspected that Ty's arrival had saved his brother Kee and two women. The fact that Ty knew where to find his brother could mean he was involved or that he followed Kee. Instead of wanting the truth, Beth was disturbed to learn she hoped he had tracked his brother to the holding house.

"How did you know where to find Kee and Hauser?" she asked.

"Call him and then you can ask him yourself."

Ty took possession of the shirt. Beth did not remove her hand, and his fell on top of hers. He met her eyes and his expression held a warning as if he knew what would happen if she didn't move away. That attraction was there again, despite his pallor and tight-lipped expression. His eyes flamed and his gaze dropped to her lips.

"You've got my cooperation, Beth. You can't convict me of helping Kee. You want the story, he'll tell you, but call him before I bleed all over my clean floor."

Droplets of blood had already landed, spattering outward evenly in all directions, looking like one of the many crime scenes she had investigated.

She lifted her phone from her back pocket and called Kee Redhorse, identified herself as Ty's new girlfriend and relayed the situation before disconnecting. "He's on his way."

The compression bandage seemed to be doing its job. No more blood ran in rivulets down his smooth ochre skin.

"Do you want me to wash off some of that blood?" she asked.

"Is that code for taking a blood sample?"

He was quick, she'd give him that.

"That ship has sailed."

"Then knock yourself out."

She went to his sink, got a dish towel and returned with a basin of warm soapy water. She dipped the cloth and wrung away the excess water before beginning at the farthest rivulets of blood. His stomach muscles twitched at the first contact and then braced. As a result, his abdomen turned to ridges of taut muscle. His jaw muscles bunched as his eyes met hers and she read the heat. Her body responded and her hand shook as she continued to wash away the blood.

"Am I hurting you?"

"More than you can ever imagine." His voice trembled.

Her smile was part grimace. He was not hers. She needed to keep reminding herself of that. But as the cloth moved over his warm skin, she ignored what was and imagined what might be. Beth took the time and trouble to memorize the patterns on his skin, the tiny mole under his armpit and the scar on his rib cage. The water in the basin turned pink as she worked. The cloth offered little barrier because she let her fingertips graze his torso, stomach and chest. The pads of her fingers relayed the electric excitement that snapped and arced like a power line ripped from its anchors by a violent storm. The storm in Ty's eyes raged as he watched her, one hand clenched to the wadded T-shirt at his shoulder. His free hand rested on his knee, fingers clamping down as if struggling not to touch her.

She worked up his arm, noting again the stylized *W* of inked feathers as she wiped the body art clean. Lower on that arm was the familiar tattoo of the US Marines Corps. As a former army captain, she had her prejudices against his branch of the armed services. But he had her respect because he'd served in Iraq and earned a rank equal to hers in half the time.

"Why didn't you stay?" she said, fingering the tattoo.

"In the marines?" He blew out a breath. "Needed at home."

"Your mother had remarried. Kee was in his residency. Colt was in the service. How where you needed?"

"Discharged."

"What?"

"Colt was discharged."

Oh, now she understood. Colt's records indicated that he had been in Walter Reed with PTSD after capture by Afghanistan insurgents.

"You left the service to bring Colt home?"

He nodded.

Again, an honorable thing to do.

"And you dove through a window for Kee." She shook her head, not wanting to change her assumptions, even when faced with new information. "And you fought Chino for me."

"Didn't do it for you," he said, and looked away, turning his attention to Hemi, who poked at his free hand until he rested it on his dog's square head. Hemi pressed her jaw to Ty's leg and looked up at him with soulful eyes.

"No?" she asked, moving to his back.

Ty glanced over his shoulder at her. "If you're blown, I'd have to do a lot more than bash Chino in the head."

"You'd have to leave."

"Only I can't because if they find out who and what you are, it's not just me. It's my whole family. You understand? It's why I didn't want this deal."

And she thought he'd been reluctant because he didn't want to risk his own neck or because it would endanger his pals. Now she understood that those men weren't his friends. They were using him and Ty was trapped. Ty had plenty of skin in this game. She was going for accolades and position. He was trying to keep his family safe. Beth wondered if she'd be able to get him free.

"I do understand," she said.

Ty was getting under her skin. She was starting to admire him, and that was just bad all around. He was her informant, and his help allowed her access to members of the Wolf Posse. Any relationship between them was impossible.

Still, she brushed his loose straight black hair away, exposing the nape of his neck. She didn't need to touch his hair but took advantage of the excuse. He did not object as she washed the juncture of his neck and shoulder, around the compression bandage and down his back. She took her time, smiling as she watched his skin pucker.

It was the last week in October and fall had arrived in the mountains, turning the leaves yellow. But it was warm in his upstairs apartment. Still, he shivered at her touch.

"You going to kiss me or just tease me?" he asked.

She dropped the dishcloth into the basin as irritation flared. He'd called her bluff.

"Is that what you want?" she asked.

She threaded her damp fingers in his hair.

"What I want you can't give me," he said.

"What's that?"

"A way out that doesn't get me or anyone I love killed."

"I'll keep you safe," she purred.

"Beth, you are the exact opposite of safe," he said.

The temptation was nearly irresistible. He reached with one hand and captured her behind the neck, drawing her in for a kiss.

"You going to stop me or kiss me again?" he asked. Was that hope in his voice, the slight strain and breathlessness?

She pressed her free hand to his chest, feeling his heartbeat pounding too fast and too hard.

"The last kiss was business."

He held her gaze. "Keep telling yourself that."

"I can control myself if you can."

His smile was all challenge. Beth's hands slid around his neck until she splayed them at the base of his skull, tilting his head back and angling it to receive her kiss. He offered no resistance as her mouth moved over his. This time their kiss was a slow sensual exploration. The heat was there, burning like a wildfire, just over the ridge, the smoke visible as the flames approached. His tongue slid against hers, and her breathing and pulse went haywire.

She was in trouble. Beth recognized that a moment

before she closed her eyes and gave herself over to his sensual assault.

Hemi scrambled to her feet, toenails scraping on the tile. She growled, hackles going up. Beth drew away and reached for her pistol. The sound of an engine reached them and then silence.

Chapter Eleven

"Kee," said Ty, guessing at the identity of their guest.

Beth moved to the side of the kitchen window, peering out at the wide driveway, weapon drawn. There was a dark pickup truck parked there. The cab light flicked on and the driver disembarked.

"How do you know?"

"I rebuilt that engine and haven't had a chance to fix the hole in his muffler. Blue 2004 RAM pickup, right?"

That looked right, she thought, eyes on the man standing beside his truck. He was the right size and build for Dr. Kee Redhorse.

The visitor turned back to his truck and withdrew a nylon bag. He looped the wide strap over his shoulder.

"Medical bag," she said. The man looked up toward the house, illuminated now by both the cab light and the automatic sensor spotlight that tripped upon his arrival.

It was Kee Redhorse. He waved and headed for the stairs. Beth tucked away her sidearm. "Remember, I'm your new girl."

"New? You sound like I have a lot of them."

"Don't you?" A man as handsome as Ty could have many.

"I'm selective."

Ty's phone rang and he lifted the mobile from his back pocket. Beth saw the caller ID. It was his younger brother, Jake Redhorse, the tribal police officer.

His voice was loud and animated enough for her to be able to hear him clearly.

"Where are you?" asked Jake.

"Home. Why? What's up?"

"Nothing. Just on a call."

"Where?" Two vertical lines etched Ty's forehead.

Jake did not answer.

"I've got to go."

"Jake?" Ty's voice held a warning as his scowl deepened and he rose to his feet, holding both the phone and the compression bandage. "Jake?" he barked, and then stared at the phone, which indicated the call had ended. Ty swore at the same time Kee knocked on Ty's kitchen door.

Beth moved to admit Dr. Redhorse, but now she was frowning, too. It seemed clear that Officer Redhorse thought his brother might be somewhere he was not supposed to be. But where?

"Responding to the fight at the roadhouse?" she asked as she turned the knob, admitting Kee.

"They'd never call the police after a simple fight like that. Chino wasn't even unconscious."

"You kicked him kind of hard."

Ty smiled as if savoring the memory. Beth frowned and opened his kitchen door to Ty's brother.

Kee looked from Ty to her. Ty's older brother was shorter and his build was leaner than Ty's and his brow was thicker. Their jawlines matched but not their noses because Kee's was longer. Kee dressed like a professional in loafers, Dockers and a blazer worn over a collared button-down shirt. Ty sat topless in jeans and biker boots with a bloody shirt pressed to his injury.

"Kee, this is Beth. She's a new friend of mine."

Kee offered her a nod but then hurried toward his brother.

"Girlfriend, according to Ma," he said to Ty.

"She called you?"

"I don't think you were even out of the drive."

Kee rummaged in his medical bag, which opened at the top like an oversize nylon cooler.

"Let's see," he said, and Ty lifted the sticky T-shirt to reveal the clotting blood and gaping wound.

"You tore out my stitches." Kee sounded put out.

"How did he do that?" Kee asked Beth.

She glanced to Ty, who shook his head.

"I'm not his keeper," she said.

"He needs one," said Kee.

Kee readied his supplies, taking out bottles and packets. Very quickly, he wiped down the injured flesh with a yellow-brown wash that Beth knew was a Betadine solution.

"You want Novocain?" he asked Ty.

"No. That stuff hurts worse than the stitches."

Kee shrugged and then, grim-faced, pulled together the ragged torn flesh and sutured the wound. When he finished he bandaged his shoulder and gave Ty a prescription for antibiotics. "Take some acetaminophen."

.   Ty rose as Kee packed up. "Some what?"

"Tylenol." Kee handed over several square sample packets of pills.

Ty walked Kee to the door and down the stairs, preceded by Hemi. Beth watched them speaking beside Kee's truck for several minutes before Kee left. She heard the noise caused by the hole in the muffler as he pulled out.

When Ty returned to the kitchen, she had the basin cleaned and set to dry in the empty dish rack. "You remembered our agreement includes telling no one who I am."

Ty pinched each side of his nose and then dropped his arm to his side. "Why would I do anything to drag my brother into the mess he's just gotten clear of?"

Kee Redhorse had been one of two prime suspects in the abduction cases. It turned out to be the work of his mentor, Hector Hauser, and his administrative assistant and mistress, Betty Mills. Hector had left a mess, which included a community whose trust was shaken, a wife with three grown daughters overshadowed by the shame of their father's actions and a tribe still trying to find the four women who were still missing. Elsie Weaver was the first taken, last November, though the two recovered kidnap victims had never seen her. Kacey Doka had escaped and reported that she had been held with Marta Garcia, Brenda Espinoza and Maggie Kesselman.

Beth knew that finding those surrogates would be the break she needed to get a promotion and her ticket out of the Oklahoma office forever. Ty had been right about why they picked her. It had been her good luck that they'd needed a woman with membership in an Apache tribe. It might have taken her five or six more years to make the kind of case that had been handed to her.

Now if she could just ignore the crackle of fire between herself and Ty Redhorse, she might get through this with a commendation, promotion and transfer orders.

Sleeping with Ty was tempting, but she wasn't going to jeopardize all that she had worked for to have him. No man was worth that. He seemed to know she would be watching, because he turned to look up at her and cast her a wicked smile that made her breath catch just as it would in the instant between when you realize you have triggered a trip wire and the moment it explodes.

He stood without his shirt, the elastic of his white underwear pressed against the flat skin of his stomach.

"I'm going to grab a shirt." He thumbed toward the hall. "You ready to turn in?"

TY FELT MANY things at that moment, his shoulder throbbing from the stitches, his skin tingling from where Beth had washed him, the restriction of his jeans against the erection that he hoped she didn't notice and the dryness in his throat when he thought of sleeping with her. Most of all he felt his heart jumping around in his chest as if on a trampoline.

"I only have the one bedroom," he said.

She thumbed toward his lopsided couch. "I'll take that."

He frowned. That would be better, easier for him, surely. But she was supposed to be his girl.

"I've never had a woman over here who slept on the couch," he said.

She smiled. "First time for everything."

He shook his head. She didn't understand.

"I'll wager you never had an FBI field agent sleep over, either," she joked.

"Exactly. My girlfriend, my *real* girlfriend, would sleep in my bedroom. A narc would sleep on that." He pointed to the sofa.

"Who's going to see me?" she asked.

He shrugged and instantly regretted it. "Anyone who comes up those stairs."

Beth glanced to the curtainless front door and frowned. The line between her eyebrows and the slight thrust of her bottom lip, paired with the look of concentration, made his skin itch. Were those goose bumps? He glanced at the hairs lifting up on his forearms and then rubbed them back down.

"That happen a lot? Folks at your door?" she asked, still facing the door.

"Folks break down. They show up here. Sometimes it's the posse. I never know."

"So why don't you have a curtain?"

"Never needed that kind of privacy before. Nothing to hide means no reason to break in."

Why did his body act as if he was about to perform a bungee jump instead of fall into bed? She wasn't going to sleep with him. He knew it. His brain knew it. His body was irrationally hopeful.

She turned to him, meeting him with those sage green eyes. "Can't we tack up a curtain?"

"Go ahead." He turned toward the hallway. "Just never did that before."

She had a hand on the back of her neck now and was frowning at the door.

"What's wrong?" he asked.

"It's the small stuff that gives away undercover operations, tips off the criminals. Like an unfamiliar car or an uncharacteristic unease in a colleague. Somebody sweating that shouldn't be."

"Or a curtain?" he asked.

"Yes. Or a darn curtain." She lowered her chin. "Your bed's big enough for two."

She'd seen it, he was sure, because he'd given her ample time to snoop around his place.

"I've always thought so."

She met his teasing smile with a glare. Agent Hoosay was not happy.

"I'll sleep on the floor," she said.

"Hemi sleeps on the floor. Or at least she starts on the floor."

He motioned to the room, then followed her as she carried her duffel down the hall that had his bathroom, small bedroom and linen closet on one side and his bedroom on the other. He waited behind her as she stood in the doorway. He knew what she saw. The queen-sized bed pushed up between the window on the back wall with a small table and lamp on one side. A reading chair with floor lamp and, opposite, the dresser drawers.

Beth's hands went to her hips. "Great."

Hemi nudged past her, dragging her living-room dog bed in her jaws. She laid it by the side of the bed where the other end table would have been. Then she abandoned her bed and claimed her spot in the center of Ty's.

"Fabulous," said Beth.

Hemi could act as a living barrier between them. In the past, when Ty had company, Hemi stayed in the living room, but tonight, he thought her presence was just the reminder Ty needed to stay on his own side of the bed.

"You take window side," said Beth, as if it was her bedroom.

"Yes, ma'am."

Beth retrieved her duffel bag and headed to the bathroom across the hall. He heard the sound of water running in the sink and wondered if she'd know where to find the fresh towels. When the shower clicked on he sat on the bed beside Hemi and pictured Beth naked, with rivulets of hot water gliding over her taut, slim body. Hemi laid her head on his thigh and sighed. Ty felt the same way.

The door across the hall finally opened and steam

billowed into the hall. It brought to him hot, wet air with the earthy scent of ginger and the fragrance of orchids.

She stepped into view. Hemi lifted her head and stared with Ty. If he had a tail it would have been thumping, as well. Beth wore a loose-fitting pink T-shirt with a scooped neck and black cotton yoga pants that stretched over her hips and her long legs, ending below the knee. From there on it was all rich golden-brown skin and slender feet. Her toes curled at his inspection, gripping the floorboards in the hall. Her toenails were painted an unexpected shocking hot pink. The color was so different from the cool, confident agent and hinted at a whimsy he had not seen. He lifted his gaze to meet hers. Her eyes held challenge.

"You don't like pink?" she asked.

"I love pink, especially on you."

She smiled. "Your turn. I set the shower temperature to cold."

So much for hoping she didn't notice his excitement. His mouth twisted downward and he wiped his sweating palms on the cotton covering his thighs. The movement made his shoulder twinge and he flinched.

Her expression changed to one of concern. The look made his heart twist. This was what it would be like to have a woman like this care what happened to him. So many choices he'd made in his life had led him here, to this place and time. He knew a confident, self-sufficient woman like Beth would not be interested in him or would be interested for all the wrong reasons. But that look almost seemed as if she cared.

"Do you need help removing that bandage?"

"I'll manage. Can't get it wet for a day or two anyway."

"Did you take anything for the pain?" she asked.

"Not yet." He didn't say that his favored medication was in the bathroom.

"It's in there, isn't it? The BC Powder?" she asked, thumbing back toward the hall. Her movement made it clear that she wore nothing beneath that T-shirt.

His gaze strayed and he watched her nipples tighten to buds beneath the thin fabric.

"You didn't take the medication your brother gave you?"

"It doesn't do anything for me."

He rose from the bed. Their eyes met. Heat flared between them, and his skin began to itch.

"I'll get them for you," she offered.

"I can do it." He didn't want to be babied. He just wanted to get through this unlikely partnership without doing something stupid, like forgetting he was a job to her.

Beth turned back at the same time he tried to step past. Her elbow collided with his biceps and he gave a hiss of pain through his teeth.

"Oh, I'm sorry!" She had a hold of his opposite arm now, helping him straighten as she looked up at him with that adorable worried expression. Now Ty's stomach hurt worse than his shoulder. Beth was killing him. She hurried to the bathroom medicine cabinet, her scent filling his nostrils as she went. Her wet hair was a riot of curls and he wanted to press his mouth to her neck and thread his fingers in her thick wonderful hair as he breathed her in.

Instead, he clenched his teeth and headed with Hemi to the kitchen, for a glass of water. She arrived with the BC Powder, his go-to for all body pain, as he was letting Hemi out.

"Extra-strength okay?" She held up the package.

"Fine."

She offered him a papery envelope of ground pain reliever in her open palm. His fingers swept over her hand, and Beth's hand trembled. His eyes lifted to hers and she lowered her lashes as green eyes darted away. He unfolded one end of the packet and poured the bitter powder to the back of his throat, then chased it with cold water.

Her upper teeth clamped over her plump bottom lip and dragged over the tender flesh. He took another long swallow of water and his throat still felt dry. There was a definite lump lodged there.

"Wow," he said. "You are something because I can't think about anything but kissing you again."

Her eyes rounded and she backed toward the hall.

"Shower," she said. "Because I am sleeping with you, but we are not having sex."

"Tonight," he said, qualifying.

"Ever. It's a job. After I bust up this surrogate ring, I am moving on and you're staying where you have always been, here on Turquoise Canyon with your family."

"Between my family and the Wolf Posse, you mean."

"What?"

"It's why I've stayed."

"You saying you are here to protect them?"

He did not reply, just walked past her down the hall. He'd already said too much. He thought about the information that Faras had given him about the location of the first ever meth lab on tribal land. He didn't like it, but it wasn't his business and it wasn't Beth's, either, because despite their agreement, this was not part of the surrogate kidnapping ring. Faras was hedging his bets, because it was very possible that the Russians would find their little fertile field of young surrogates ruined by the increasing attention of the police and federal authorities.

Ty was angry over the fact that the Russian crime organization supposed that no one would miss the girls that disappeared and even more furious that they were right. Up until Jake and his new wife, Lori, made the connection between the disappearances and the tribe's clinic, no one had thought these missing girls were anything more than runaways.

Ty hit the shower, careful not to soak the bandage Kee had fixed to his shoulder. The stitches tugged, but he managed to get himself clean and ready for bed. He dragged on a pair of loose sweatpants and shuffled like an old man across the hall. Beth was in bed under the sheets and blanket. Hemi stretched out on top of the blanket beside her like a living partition. Ty no longer cared. He was too tired to do anything more than imagine having a woman as smart and beautiful as Beth pressed up beside him in his bed. He realized that living above his garage was not likely what she pictured when she closed her eyes and that conjecture took some of the spark from him. Hemi fell asleep first, snoring as usual. Beth fell asleep next, likely with her hand on her service pistol.

Ty waited for the medication to take the sharpest notes of pain from his shoulder and then he closed his eyes, drifting away to sleep. His dreams were filled with a sense of looming menace that woke him in a sweat during the night. He wondered if he had a fever. Hemi lifted her head and then dropped it on his stomach. He rested a hand on her shoulder and noticed that Beth was lying on her side facing him. One of her hands was on the dog's rib cage, just inches from his. In sleep, her skin glowed ethereal, like a fairy queen's, and her face was as serene and calm as the clear night sky. He resisted the urge to touch his fingers to hers and closed his eyes. The beat of his heart echoed in his healing shoulder.

The next thing he knew he was startled awake a few hours later by an unfamiliar ringtone. He threw himself to a seated position as Beth scrambled off the bed and retrieved her mobile phone, which she had plugged into a charger on his dresser. He scooped up his mobile from the nightstand and saw that it wasn't even 6:00 a.m. He'd been asleep less than five hours.

Ty sank back to the pillows and groaned, covering his eyes with his arm against the pale gray light that filtered through the slats of the blinds. His shoulder pulsed to life, sending a dull ache down his arm with each heartbeat.

Beth was speaking to her supervisor. She was telling him she could be there in twenty minutes. When she finished the call she was scrambling through her duffel.

"Be where in twenty?" he asked.

"Go back to sleep," she said.

"Yeah, right. Am I going?"

She shook her head, her arms now full of clothing and her bathroom bag. "I'll see you later today. Just carry on as you normally would do."

"So fix the carburetor. Is that your suggestion?"

But she was already gone.

He was still in bed when she returned. She was dressed as a civilian, her brown leather coat hiding her shoulder harness and her black turtleneck sweater hiding the FBI shield he suspected she wore. "Call me if you hear anything from Faras."

"Yes, Agent Hoosay."

Hemi stood before Beth, tail wagging.

"Let her out?" she asked.

"If you wouldn't mind."

Beth and Hemi disappeared down the hall and Ty rose to meet the day. He was on his second cup of coffee when Hemi demanded readmission and breakfast. Ty spent Monday morning in the shop and the afternoon took Hemi over to his mother's place. Ty fixed her bathroom sink drain, which was choking under the strain of hair shed by the three foster girls, Lori's sisters, and his own sister, Abbie. He pulled a wad of wet black hair the size of a drowned rat from the drain, solving the problem.

His mother thanked him in the usual way by fixing him a sandwich. But she sat with him, waiting until he finished to bring up whatever it was that was troubling her. Then she pushed a folded sheet of paper at him with the warning to not get upset.

He unfolded the page and noted the prison insignia at the top of the letterhead. His heart rate doubled as he scowled. He was already upset.

When she spoke, his mother's voice held a familiar tightness he had not heard in a long time. "He's been paroled."

Chapter Twelve

There was no need to ask who Ty's mother meant. His father had served seven years on a ten-year sentence. They'd all been bracing for this. Seven years ago, Ty had thought he had everything settled. Addie would be in college, hopefully, and Ty would have his brothers to help protect their mother.

But Colt was gone. And Kee and Jake both had their own families to protect.

"When?" asked Ty.

"Soon. I don't know exactly. I put in a postconviction request form so they'll notify me fifteen days before release, but you know, the mail up here is slow. Might not know right away."

Ty glanced down at the letter again and realized that it was over a month old. "You just got this?"

His mother flushed. "No. A while ago."

"And you didn't tell me until now?"

"I knew you'd be upset."

That didn't even begin to cover it. Ty had been to see his father only once after he was incarcerated because he wanted to see him locked up. Only after

the visit did Ty realize the vanity of that meeting and
the danger it brought. Colton Redhorse had figured it
out at first glance. His father was a brutal man with a
hairpin trigger. He'd raged and the guards had come.
Ty had not gone back. He didn't need to. The damage
was already done.

His father was as unpredictable as a tornado. And
just like with a tornado, Ty knew he would cause de-
struction, but there was really no way to predict where
or when. "Do Jake and Kee know?"

"I didn't know how to tell them. I haven't even
told Burt yet." She'd told Ty before her own husband.

Ty's intake of breath was sharp. Both Jake and Kee
visited their father on occasion. It had been Kee who
had related to Ty that Colton had discovered that May
had remarried, and his father had not taken the news
well. Burt was in serious danger.

"But he won't come here," said May, her head bob-
bing as she tried to convince herself.

Ty met her gaze, offering no reassurance. He knew
that his father would strive not to get caught. But he
highly doubted he would resist the urge to hurt Burt
and the woman he still considered his wife, divorce
papers aside.

"Your father isn't stupid, Ty," said his mother. "He
doesn't want to go back there."

"That doesn't mean he won't hurt you, Mom. He
knows you won't press charges."

"It only makes things worse," she said, defending her position.

And here he was, right back where he'd been when

he was eighteen, trying to protect his mother, brothers and sister from his father. Only this time, his father would see Ty coming.

Going to the police would do nothing. His father had served his time and Ty knew that tribal could act only after his father committed a crime. By then it would be too late.

He needed to speak to Faras. Again. Damn.

Ty made his excuses to his mother and broke the news to Burt about the firestorm heading their way. Burt went pale. He was a good-hearted man, but not a fighter. Ty cautioned Burt to contact him if they received any more information on his father's imminent parole. Then he whistled for Hemi, who crawled out from under his mother's front porch and stretched. Ty opened the passenger door and folded back the seat, waiting for his dog to climb in. Then they drove directly to the Wolf Posse's headquarters.

The gang had moved up in the world since their affiliation with the Russian crime syndicate. They no longer lived in a hollowed-out shell of a building. Faras had purchased a ranch outside the town of Koun'nde with cash. The outfit was fenced with an electric gate entry. The only one on the reservation, as far as Ty knew. Once beyond this first security barrier, Ty passed two checkpoints, although only one would have been visible to outsiders. When he was within sight of the barn and house, he was greeted by the first sentry. Today it was Henry Lavender, who stepped off the porch and raised a hand at Ty in greeting, waiting for the dust to settle before approaching his car. Ty lowered his front window with the crank.

"Hey, Ty. Heard about the fight with Chino. Man! You messed up his face. He had to go to the dentist in Darabee. He been gone for hours." Henry offered Hemi his hand and then scratched behind the dog's ears while Hemi lifted her chin and let her eyes roll back in her head. "She likes that," said Lavender, grinning.

Ty stuck with the topic of conversation—Chino and the dentist. "Maybe we'll get lucky and they'll wire Chino's jaw shut."

Henry snorted with laughter, holding his fist to his mouth to stifle his mirth. He glanced over his shoulder at the closed door as if checking to see if anyone had noticed his hilarity. Then he shifted his gaze back to Ty.

Ty stepped from the '67 GTO and signaled Hemi to stay put.

"Faras here?" Ty asked.

"Yeah, but he's in some kind of meeting. Something's happening, bro. I heard them mention Quinton. They didn't sound happy."

"What about him?"

"Dunno. Something bad, you ask me."

"Tell him I'm here. I'll wait."

Henry nodded and ducked into the house. Ty glanced about at the trucks and cars parked along the drive. He had worked on most of them. He recognized Faras's second car, a new black Mustang. He studied the cars he did not know. He wondered if any belonged to the Russian connection.

Today he was here about his own business. Business that concerned Faras as much as himself. Dangerous business. But if the opportunity arose to learn some information about the missing women from his tribe, he was not above taking advantage.

Henry returned after a few minutes and ushered him in through the living room, where Norleena Caddo and Autumn Tay lounged on the overstuffed sofa watching a reality TV show involving women as overly primped and made up as the two of them. Ty paused to issue a greeting in Tonto, which they both returned without shifting their eyes from the large-screen plasma TV. Both women were in their early twenties, pretty if you wiped off the paint smearing their faces, and both had joined the gang during high school. They reminded him of Japanese geisha, here to entertain and attend to the men and, equally, to stay out of their way when unwanted. Ty compared their vapid expressions to the purpose he saw glimmering in Beth Hoosay's bright eyes. Were there gangs where she lived in Oklahoma? Did she have a solid home life that helped her avoid such land mines and trapdoors?

As he entered the dining room, he made a mental note to find out more about her past. She interested him and he thought it would be to his benefit to know more about where she came from.

Faras sat at the head of the rectangular wooden table. He motioned for Andre Napualani to move over and make room for Ty. Also at the table were two other members of his posse, Deoma Quintero and Eldon Kahn. Noticeable in his absence was Quinton Ford. And Chino Aria, of course, though Ty knew where he was today and the knowledge that Chino was in a dentist's chair gave him some measure of satisfaction.

Ty took the seat vacated by Andre. Despite what his brothers, his mother, his father and tribal police believed, Ty was not a member of the Wolf Posse. Perhaps he was in a worse position because he owed Faras. But Faras also owed Ty. Friends since high school, the two had a sort of symbiotic relationship forged by need, mutual respect and common history.

"You want something to drink, Ty?" asked Faras.

"Dr Pepper."

Faras called to Norleena Caddo to fetch the drink. A moment later Norleena clicked through the dining room on ridiculously high heels that were as impractical as her short shorts and halter top. The men watched as she opened the refrigerator and then leaned over as if knowing all eyes were upon her. She retrieved the soft drink and used the edge of the counter to pop off the cap with practiced expertise. Then she returned, swaying her hips, and slid the drink before Ty. Her mission completed, she rested a hand on Faras and asked if he needed anything else. Ty always felt nauseated at the displays of submission required by the females in the gang. Their compliance was mandatory. However, he noted that the pecking order between females was much less civilized. Some of the battles for dominance were epic. Most recently, the removal of the alpha female, Minnie Cobb, had left a power vacuum. Much as Noreen would like the spot, Ty knew that it was Jewell Tasa who seemed to be stepping into Minnie's expensive shoes.

Faras gave Noreen a pat on the posterior and pushed her back toward the living room. Then he watched her go. Only when she was out of sight did they return to business.

"Happy to see you, bro," said Faras.

"I'm sorry about Chino," said Ty.

"Had it coming. She wasn't one of ours and you told him she was your girl. Listen, we've had some trouble. I need to finish up with my council. You got any business for me?" asked Faras.

Ty appreciated Faras seeing him without notice and interrupting his own business for Ty. It was the kind of respect he did not afford anyone else, except his bosses, the drug distribution network and now the Russians. Ty got right to the point.

"My dad's parole came through." Ty watched as some of the color drained from Faras's face.

"That so?"

Ty nodded, holding his friend's gaze and seeing the worry there. Faras understood that his father's release threatened them both.

"Yeah, we need to talk. Meet you out by the fire pit in ten."

Dismissed, Ty left the council table.

"You want company?" asked Faras, motioning his head to the living room.

Ty swallowed back his disdain. "Naw. Not today."

Or any day. Ty didn't want a woman who was obliged to service him like he was some John. The entire practice sickened him almost as much as knowing that Faras chose who would be initiated each year, just as he picked which girls would disappear. Faras knew the tribe in a way that even their own tribal council didn't. He knew who was vulnerable and who was not, who would be missed and who would not. He'd chosen well, but he hadn't counted on the resourcefulness of two of his victims.

Zella Colelay had evaded capture by his posse for long enough to deliver the baby forced upon her. And a second victim, Kacey Doka, had escaped capture to prove she had not been a runaway. And that had been a problem that could not be erased.

TY SAT UNDER the newly erected pergola beside the circular masonry fire pit. He did not attend the Wolf Posse parties. He avoided this house whenever possible and met Faras only in the relatively neutral ground of the roadhouse. But today he made the exception because his father would be coming home to Turquoise Canyon.

It was another twenty minutes before Faras appeared carrying an open beer bottle. He sat in the shade beside Ty.

It was a common way in his culture to speak around issues. The proper way to address a concern was to sneak up on it casually after some degree of small talk. But Faras was a businessman and rarely had time for custom.

"Before we get to your dad, I want to tell you about Quinton."

"What about him?"

Faras leaned forward, gripping the neck of the bottle with both hands as he stared at the dirt before his boots. Then he shook his head, his lips a tight line.

Ty leaned forward as well, though the action hurt his shoulder. "Faras? Did something happen?"

"Yeah." His voice was hushed. "Well, it hasn't happened yet. But it will." Faras shook his head. He was not usually this obtuse. Then without warning Faras lifted the full beer bottle and threw it with all his might. The bottle sailed in a graceful arc, spinning end over end as it expelled its contents before smashing on the masonry.

Ty sat back, waiting.

"There was a raid on our meth lab."

"Deer Kill Meadow?" asked Ty, repeating the location of the lab that Faras had mentioned to him previously. Faras had also told Ty that he would be responsible for making deliveries from that meth lab. Ty had been thinking of ways to get out of that. Now, however, with his father's imminent release, his bargaining position was greatly compromised.

"No, no, man. That's the point. Ain't no lab on Deer Kill Meadow. Just like there ain't no lab down on Canyon Ridge Road."

"What?" Ty didn't understand.

Faras turned in his seat to face Ty. "We ain't got a meth lab, bro. Neither place. Made it up."

Ty felt his skin tingling as he recalled how close he

had come to telling Beth about the lab. But it wasn't related to their case and he hadn't made an agreement to help with anything but the surrogate ring. Then he remembered the early morning phone call and Beth's hasty departure. Was that the tip from Quinton reaching the FBI here on Turquoise Canyon? Ty clenched his fists and forced himself to remain still as his muscles twitched and his skin prickled.

Was she all right?

"Why?"

"A test," said Faras. Finally, he met Ty's gaze. "I should have known it wasn't you. But I had to be sure. You've been different since Jake found that baby. Distant. I knew you didn't like our association with the Russians and I knew we had a leak. Someone told the FBI where to find Kacey. You delivered her and she was your brother's girl, so you seemed the obvious choice. And then someone told the FBI where to find the two girls they were keeping at Antelope Lake. Your brother Kee was there with Dr. Hauser. I thought it likely that Kee had told your brother Jake about the location of the house. But I know your brother Kee and, no offense, he could not have overtaken those Russian soldiers. I still don't know what happened except that Hauser and the two watching over our goods all died."

Ty did not like hearing the captured women being referred to as goods. He had a sister about the same age as the missing girls and it burned him up inside to think of someone doing that to Addie.

"So I set up you and Quinton," continued Faras.

"Fed you each a different location. Today the FBI raided the house on Canyon Ridge."

Ty needed to speak to Beth. To warn her. Was it just a test or also a trap? What if Faras's men saw her and remembered her?

If Faras knew Beth's identity, then she was dead and he would follow soon after.

Suddenly, it was hard to sit still. He longed to reach for his phone and call her. Hear her voice and be certain she was safe. Instead he laced his hands before him and told himself not to let Faras see that he was nervous or that his shoulder was injured. He was grateful for the leather jacket he wore over the injury earned while helping Kee rescue Ava Hood at Antelope Lake.

"Quinton?" asked Ty.

"Yeah. My second. Can you believe that? I hope they paid him well and he put something away for his woman and kid because he's not coming home to them."

Ty's heart hammered. "No?"

"Minute I got the call about the raid, I sent out Chino."

Chino was not at the dentist's. He was assigned to murder Quinton. Ty's ears buzzed. He liked Quinton. He'd almost been Quinton.

"I'm sorry," said Ty. His throat felt as hard and dry as a canyon wall.

"I need a new second."

"Chino wants that job," said Ty.

"And you don't. But the Russians are pulling out

and when they go, so does the money. They're used to it now, my guys. Food, booze, nice wheels, you know? It won't be easy replacing that kind of income. We need to prepare for that. Besides, Chino don't want to be my second. He wants to be alpha wolf."

"They're pulling out?" Ty tried to keep the elation from his voice. The scourge among them was leaving. Jake and the FBI had done it, put enough pressure on the organized crime bosses that the Russians were leaving their rez. His brother Colt could come back home. Ty could have danced, he was so happy. "What about the ones they still have?"

"They own them. Use them again or send them into service some other way." He shrugged. "Dunno."

Human trafficking, Ty realized. That was what Faras was saying. "They're our women."

"They're like Peter Pan's lost boys. The ones that fell out of their strollers and no one noticed or cared. Remember you read me that story?" Faras grinned.

Ty had a sickening feeling that the very sad and lost boy he'd read that story to had grown up to be a pirate himself and used that tale to influence his selection of victims.

"We should demand them back," said Ty.

"You don't ask those guys for nothing. They'll hand you your ass and make you wear it as a hat. Besides, we got our own troubles. Your dad is coming back. We have to be strong because sure as hell, he'll challenge me. I need you as my second, Ty. I want you to join us again."

Chapter Thirteen

Beth returned to Ty's place after sundown on Monday night to find the bay doors of the shop open and Hemi trotting out to meet her. The dog escorted her down the drive, barking joyfully but not getting too close to her motorcycle. She cut the engine as Ty stepped out of the garage, using a rag to wipe his greasy hands.

The day had been terrible. The tip was bad, the location wrong and the result was that fifteen heavily armed FBI agents had startled a very nice older couple from their bed. The rest of the day had been spent making apologies and trying and failing to bring in their informant, Quinton Ford.

There had also been a break in the surrogacy case. Police in Santa Fe, New Mexico, had picked up Elsie Weaver, the first of the women to go missing. Beth's supervisor had flown out there and discovered that Elsie had never been abducted. According to the sixteen-year-old, she had been to the clinic in November of last year but that visit had nothing to do with her decision to run away with her twenty-three-year-old boyfriend, now being held in the Santa Fe jail on a growing list of charges.

Beth had gone back to Betty Mills, the former health clinic administrator and Dr. Hauser's accomplice there. Mills had been transferred to the larger facility in the neighboring city of Darabee. Betty had been less than cooperative. Her plea deal had gone out the window when she failed to mention that tribal police detective Ava Hood's cover had been blown. Mills had let Hood walk right into a trap that nearly got her killed. Eventually, Mills verified for Beth that Elsie Weaver had never been one of their girls, as Mills called her, simply the inspiration, because when Elsie disappeared, no one cared. No one looked. She was listed in a database and forgotten. That gave Hector the idea of a simple way to raise the funds he needed to bring their facility into the twenty-first century.

Hector had approached a colleague in Phoenix who ran a fertility clinic. Then a contact was made with Kuznetsov's representative. The tribe's gang was enlisted to capture and deliver, and just like that, they were in business.

Beth rolled the bike onto its kickstand and slid off the seat. Beth still did not wholly understand Ty's role in all this. He was an enigma. May Redhorse's second son was not at all what she had expected. He had clearly moved to protect his brother Kee's fiancée from her captivity and, if Officer Redhorse was to be believed, to save Jake and the infant he and his wife adopted from attack. Yet they had him on driving the recaptured Kacey Doka back to the Russians. She suspected there was more to that story than what she had read in the deposition, but they didn't need it because his blood at the crime scene was the hook that guaranteed Ty's compliance, as much as that was possible.

Ty stepped into the circle of the floodlight fixed above the bay doors. The bright light reflected off his brow, cheeks and chin. His biceps bunched as he worked the rag, and her stomach pitched and something lower thrummed. Seeing him momentarily chased away the weariness that had settled between her shoulders.

She cast him a lazy smile. He didn't return it. In fact, there was a new tension in his face and a ticking beneath his eye.

"Where's Quinton?" he asked, his voice calm, but he bunched the rag at his side. Hemi came to him, sitting at his feet. She whined, as if sensing his upset.

"How do you know about that?"

"Canyon Ridge Road. Meth lab. Right?"

Beth faced him, now completely on alert. She needed to know how Ty knew about this.

"Did anyone see you?"

"What?"

"Were you there?" He moved forward, his gaze sweeping her as if searching for injury.

Her skin tingled a warning. "I can't tell you that. Now tell me, how did you know about this?"

"They told me it was Deer Kill Meadow Road," said Ty.

"Who did?"

Ty explained it to her. Beth felt her chest squeeze. They'd thought their informant had run out on them. Intentionally fed them bad intel for his payout and then fled. The truth was much worse.

"But you signed an agreement to reveal such information," said Beth.

"No. My agreement was specific to the surrogate-ring case."

He was right and his intelligence now irritated her. She wasn't used to informants who had this kind of smarts.

"Beth, if they saw you, you're blown."

That made her pause as she thought back over her day.

"I never left the vehicle. Tinted glass," she said as much to herself as to Ty.

His shoulders sagged. "You sure?"

She nodded. That was relief in his expression and not for his own skin. Ty was concerned for hers.

"Tell me all you know about this," she said.

"They fed us each different locations to see which way you moved. Canyon Ridge Road was the location they told Quinton. You understand? Now Faras has his snitch. It's Quinton and he's sent Chino to kill him."

Beth wheeled back to the bike, pausing only to make a call. Then she was racing back to the command center they had set up in Koun'nde. They had to find Quinton before Chino Aria did.

BETH DID NOT return that night. On Tuesday, Ty tried to get Kee and Jake out for supper but only managed to get them to come for a drink. They met in the casino's sports bar. The waitress wore an elaborate purple wig, a plastic tiara and fairy wings. She took their drink orders and left them three small candy bars with the menus.

"What's up with that?" asked Ty.

"It's Halloween," said Kee. "I promised Mom I'd be home in time to take Abbie, Shirley and Shirley's brothers out trick-or-treating."

Halloween. Ty had completely forgotten. Lately, his entire life seemed a sort of trick. Ty glanced at the waitress and wondered if he should know what she was dressed as.

"What about Jackie and Winnie?" he asked, mentioning the other two foster girls staying with their mother.

Kee ticked off the children on his fingers. "Winnie is manning the door for Mom, Jackie has a party and Ava is taking the girls out." He was referring to Ava Hood's nieces, Olivia, Alexandra and Margarita, all under five. It looked very much as if Kee and Ava would take temporary custody of her nieces while Ava's sister sorted out her drinking at a six-week rehab program.

"What are they dressing as?" asked Jake.

"Princesses for the twins and Olivia is going as blue."

"Blue what?"

"I have no idea. She likes blue."

That three-year-old had ideas all her own, admitted Ty.

He waited until the waitress delivered their drinks before dropping the bombshell about their father's parole.

"Well, he won't do anything stupid, like threaten Mom, because he'll be on parole," said Kee, ever the rational and optimistic one. "If he even sets foot on her property, she can have him arrested."

"She never had him arrested before," Ty reminded him.

"I'll start the paperwork on an order of protection," said Jake.

Ty groaned. "That won't stop him."

Jake still believed in the law, even after all he'd seen. Admirable and naive, Ty thought.

Jake had once called the police on their father, assuming, wrongly, that they could help. Neighbors had called, as well. But May had, without exception, failed to press charges at every opportunity. Afraid, he now knew, of what would happen when he got out.

Jake lifted his chin and glared at Ty. "It won't stop him, but it will give me the right to arrest him if he goes near her."

Ty hissed between his teeth, letting the frustration escape like steam from an engine. "You can't be there twenty-four-seven. Eventually he'll come after her and Burt. And what about Addie? What if our sister gets between Colton and Ma?" Ty had stopped calling their father Dad the day he saw his father bounce a beer bottle off his mother's head. He'd called the police that time and paid the price.

Jake's mouth flattened and his eyes went steely.

Ty hadn't been there when his father broke their mother's arm. But Addie and Colt had been. Colt had called Jake, who was then fourteen and at basketball practice. Ty had been off with Faras somewhere causing trouble and Kee had been in his second year of medical school.

"Restraining orders only work on people who follow the law," said Ty.

"What do you suggest?" asked Kee.

Ty's reply was immediate. "One of us needs to be out there with her."

Jake's face was grim. He had a new wife and baby girl to look after. He had a full-time job that required him to be away long dangerous hours.

"Prison might have changed him," said Kee, looking for the good in people even where there was none.

"I'm sure it has," said Ty. "Made him meaner, tougher and more dangerous."

"We don't need to do anything yet," said Jake. "I'll call the parole office and ask to be contacted when his release is scheduled. In the meantime, I'll get Mom to file the paperwork."

"Good luck with that," said Ty.

"Just let me handle this," said Jake. He rubbed his neck. "Maybe I'll go pick him up. Better way to keep an eye on him. Find out what his plans are. You don't know for certain that he's coming here."

Ty did know because his father had a score to settle with Faras and with him. "He'll be back."

"Well," said Jake, "we'll see." Then he turned to Kee. "Did I hear that Ava is going back to school?"

Ava Hood, Kee's intended, had been a tribal police detective down on the rez in Salt River, but she'd broken one too many rules and lost her shield. Woman after Ty's own heart. Ava had done what it took to get her niece back. Now she and Kee had custody of Louisa Tah and her other three nieces while her sister struggled with some addiction problems. Both his brothers had full plates.

"Yes," said Kee. "Forensic fire investigator."

Sounded hard to Ty.

"Knew we wouldn't keep her in dispatch for long," said Jake. "Oh, and I heard from Bear Den that we found Elsie Weaver."

Elsie was the first to go missing and, according to what Beth had told him, the inspiration for Hector's plan to use certain women from their tribe as surrogates.

"Where?" asked Ty.

"Flagstaff. She's working down there, living with her boyfriend."

"She's okay?" asked Ty.

"Completely. She wasn't taken by anyone. She's a runaway. When they picked up her boyfriend on shoplifting, Elsie came to get him and was detained. She just wants nothing to do with her family."

"Can you blame her?" asked Ty.

Jake made a face and continued, knowing as

well as anyone what went on in the Weaver family. "They've been contacted nonetheless. She's told the police down there that she didn't know about the others."

"She coming home?" asked Kee.

Jake sighed. "She's a minor, so yes. Don't think they'll keep her long, though."

"So that leaves just three missing?" said Ty.

"Marta Garcia, Brenda Espinoza and Maggie Kesselman," said Jake.

Kee glanced at his watch. The gathering had reached its conclusion. Ty had failed to get either brother to recognize the magnitude of the threat their father posed. But that was because he had been unwilling to share one critical piece of information, the reason Colton Redhorse would be coming back looking for blood.

Chapter Fourteen

Quinton Ford's body was found on the southern bank of the Hakathi River between the Red Rock Dam and Antelope Lake sometime on the morning of Tuesday, October 31, by two kayakers. Beth had not learned this until late that afternoon when someone from the Arizona Highway Patrol notified tribal police that they'd found a body, possibly Native American. Photos had been sent and the identification made.

In other words, the body was found off the rez, making it a matter for the Arizona Highway Patrol. By the time Beth discovered that they had a body, Ford's remains had already been moved to the morgue in Darabee Hospital. Beth met with the medical examiner, who had made only a preliminary check. The ME had experience with several suicides from each of the series of four dams and told her that, based on the visible injuries, he believed the death was caused by a fall and not drowning. He said the autopsy would determine if the deceased had water in his lungs or if he survived the plunge, only to drown. Beth took charge of the records and the body, waiting until after

9:00 p.m. for someone from the Phoenix office to arrive to take custody of Quinton Ford's remains.

Beth suspected the manner of death would be listed as homicide, not suicide. The worst part, aside from having one of their informants killed, was that there was no one to notify. Quinton Ford's mother was dead. No father was listed on his birth records and he had no siblings. It seemed Ford had only the Wolf Posse, and his betrayal of that family had come with swift retribution. Now she needed to prove it.

For now, she would concentrate on the case that would get her noticed—breaking up the surrogate ring.

When she returned to Ty's home, it was after midnight. She had expected to be locked out, but saw the bay door open and the lights on.

Hemi sprinted out to meet her and escorted her in, her barking muted by the sound of Beth's bike. The dog waited until Beth cut the engine and dismounted before jumping up on her hind legs to wave her front paws in the air as if to say hello. Beth laughed and gave Hemi a scratch as she fell back to all fours.

Beth walked with Hemi to the open bay door to find Ty working in his garage. He wore jeans and a tight gray muscle shirt that revealed the white gauze now covering his shoulder injury. Sweat and grease mingled on his defined muscles, his arms raised as he worked beneath a car he had driven up onto a lift using ramps.

The mobile light, complete with cage and hook,

was fixed to the undercarriage of an automobile she recognized as belonging to his mother.

"You're going to pull out those stitches again," she said by way of greeting.

He ignored the warning and spoke without looking at her. "Busy day?"

"Yes."

"Hungry?" he asked.

She hadn't realized just how hungry she was but now recalled she completely missed dinner. "Yes."

"I've got steaks, steak fries and mini Snickers."

She lifted her brows in confusion, thinking chocolate an odd choice as a side dish.

"It's Halloween," said Ty, and glanced at the wall clock. "Or it was."

She'd been reminded by the medical examiner's necktie, which had been covered in skeletons. She really thought he could wear that any day. Beth glanced toward the road.

"You get any trick-or-treaters out here?" She looked back at the highway that threaded down the lonesome stretch between Koun'nde and Piñon Forks, thinking a kid would have to be crazy to come down this drive.

"I got them for you. Trick-or-treat," he said.

She managed a weary smile. "Have you eaten?"

He should have, hours ago, but he shook his head. "Not yet."

Had he been waiting for her? That thought pleased her far more than it should have because it made them seem like a real couple. The disturbing feeling of intertwining her work and her personal life wiped away her smile. Ty had become much more than a way in to the Wolf Posse, a way to make her case.

"Been busy," he said by way of an excuse, and headed for the stairs with Hemi at his heels.

Ty flipped on the oven to preheat it, then returned several minutes later, after showering and putting on a clean shirt. She'd managed to set the table in his absence. She offered to make a salad, but Ty had opted to just slice a head of lettuce into quarters and drizzle blue-cheese dressing over the wedges, then sprinkle bacon crumbles on top. It was all she could do to keep from scooping it off her plate and into her mouth as he dropped the frozen potato wedges onto a cookie sheet and tucked them into the oven.

She told herself that steak did not take long to cook and she could wait, as she followed him downstairs on weary legs. He turned on the gas grill, which sat tucked under the stairs. Beth rested in a lawn chair feeling like a pencil worn down to the nub. The steaks hit the hot grill with a satisfying sizzle. The smell of cooking beef made her mouth water. When she next trudged up the stairs, the kitchen was filled with the homey aroma of roasting potatoes. She sighed with pleasure.

"Beer or water?" he asked.

Beer sounded good, but she was still on duty. "Water is fine."

Ty stopped at the open refrigerator. "I have one ice tea."

"Sold," she said, raising a finger as if at an auction.

Hemi curled in her bed by the door. Clearly she did not subsist on table scraps, which was good because Beth doubted there would be any left, at least from her plate.

Ty handed over the bottle of tea and set a glass of water beside his own plate. Then he served the steak, medium rare, with Worcestershire sauce and ketchup for the fries. For the next few minutes Beth was completely occupied with the meal. She paused when she noticed Ty was not moving. She glanced up and found him smiling at her.

"Good?" he asked.

"Great. This is the best steak I've ever had."

His head tilted to the side and his eyebrows lifted in a look of skepticism.

"No. Really."

"Well, hunger makes the best spice." He lifted his fork and stared down at his plate. "I think I see why my mom still likes having us all over for Sunday dinner. There's something satisfying about feeding someone…" He seemed like he was about to say more, but his mouth snapped shut.

Someone…you cared about? Beth wondered, silently finishing the sentence. She gave him a wary smile. In another time and place he would be exactly the sort of man she would find appealing. He clearly loved his family. He worked hard. Was a risk-taker and took excellent care of his other female companion, Hemi. But the list of problems could not be overlooked. Ty had committed armed robbery at only eighteen. His father was a career criminal and abused his wife. Such things ran in families, didn't they?

"Well, it's excellent. Thank you for dinner." She returned her attention to her plate to finish the last bite of steak and the three remaining fries.

He waited until she set aside her fork and knife before speaking again.

"Snickers?" he asked.

She smiled, hands on her stomach. "No room."

Beth finished the last of her ice tea.

"Did you find Quinton?" he asked.

She lowered the bottle to the tabletop and nodded, her smile gone. "We did."

He didn't ask her if he was alive. It seemed to her that he already knew. He tucked his chin and was silent for a long time.

Finally he spoke without meeting her gaze. "Where?"

"Below Red Rock Dam."

His steady gaze seemed to accuse her of something.

"You're a witness." She stretched her hand across the table. "You can testify that Faras fed you false information."

His eyes rounded. "You didn't go to Deer Kill Meadow?"

"No. After the intel you supplied, we felt going there would compromise you."

She didn't say aloud that Quinton's death was on their hands. They had moved on the intelligence Quinton had provided, even though it had no bearing on the case they were supposed to be up here investigating, exposing him as their informant. Ty had held the information and she was so glad.

"I'm sorry about your friend," said Beth.

"He wasn't my friend. None of them are my friends."

"But…" Her words trailed off. She didn't know what to say. It seemed clear that he had chosen to join the gang at some point. He had acted on Faras's order. And he had branded himself with their sign. She glanced at the four eagle feathers forming the letter *W* on Ty's forearm. She lifted her attention to find Ty's gaze sharp and intent.

"You're a member of the posse," she said.

He did not argue. "I joined when I was eighteen. When I came back from Iraq, I partially severed that relationship. But we're still connected."

"I've never heard of anyone leaving the gang. I don't think it's possible."

"It is."

"How?"

"If I tell you something about that day I drove the getaway car with my father, can you use it against me?"

"Not on that one. Statute of limitations is up and you were offered a deal. Right?"

"Yes."

"So I can't use anything you say against you unless it is related to a crime without limitations, like murder."

Ty nodded his understanding, still not meeting her

gaze. She waited, praying that whatever he might tell her would not incriminate him, that he had never killed someone. She realized with a sinking feeling she did not want him to put her in the position to have to arrest him.

Gangs had entrance rituals. For boys it was usually crime. For girls it was sex. What crime had Ty committed to join?

His chin lifted and his eyes narrowed. The expression made him look dangerous. "I joined the Wolf Posse because of him."

"Your father?"

He nodded, sending his hair over his forehead, where it hung across his eyes.

"Why?"

"My father was the next in line to head the Wolf Posse back then. He was thirty-nine and second in command. Then Gerome Hessay was shot in a drug deal gone wrong. They lost their leader and the product. So nothing to sell. After Gerome died, my father moved to take his place. So did Faras Pike, but he was young, only twenty. The members were leaning toward my dad."

"Faras was a classmate of yours back then." Beth sat forward, interested in what he would tell her.

"Yes and no. Faras was a classmate of Kee's, but he'd been left back. He was in my grade for a year or so. Then he dropped out. Encouraged me to do the same. Almost did."

"So what happened between Faras and your dad?" she asked.

"Gang was short on funds because of the drug deal falling through. A robbery was a way for my dad to establish dominance, be the hero and fix the problem with our distributors. They don't care if we sell the drugs or lose them or smoke them, just so long as they get paid on time. I offered to drive my dad, and then I called Faras."

She sat back as the implication of what he was saying sank in. Beth met his intent stare and saw that her suspicions were correct. But she had to hear him say it. "You set up your father?"

Ty did not answer the question at first. Finally, he inclined his head, admitting it. Hard to blame him. His father was a petty crook, a known gang member, and by all reports, a brutal man.

"Faras had the police there waiting," said Ty. "Tipped them before my dad even cleared the doors of that liquor store."

"And you made sure he didn't escape. Crashed the getaway car." She should have known if for no other reason than that Ty did not crash cars. He was a good driver. No, a great one. "But you were arrested as well."

"Worth it. He broke my mother's arm that January and still she wouldn't press charges. Jake called the cops, but my dad was back the next day. So I went to Faras. Two months later my father went to prison. They blamed him for picking me. Young kid. Stupid choice for a getaway driver. And Faras became the gang's new leader."

Ty gained respect in her eyes. He'd been dealt a hard hand and done what he could.

"Why wouldn't your mom press charges?" she asked.

He rested his forehead in his hand, elbow on the table, and peered up at her as if talking about this gave him a headache. But he answered her.

"Because he said it would only be worse if she did. He threatened us, his kids, used us as collateral to keep her from leaving him."

"And you made him go away without killing him."

"For that, I would have gone to jail."

"But instead you went free."

"They let me join the US Marines."

"And you distinguished yourself."

She recognized the look of sorrow as his eyes changed the direction of their focus, drifting off to some unknown place.

So many of the pieces of the puzzle that were Ty Redhorse fell into place. Ty had used his Big Money, the portion of the tribe's revenue from the casino profits distributed to members on their 18th birthday, for Kee's education. He had provided Colt with a vintage Chevy pickup truck that was distinctive, in that the colors he chose were not the ones favored by the Wolf Posse. In fact, the only one he had not provided transportation for was his brother Jake.

"Did you want to stay away, Ty?"

His gaze drifted back to her. His jaw was set tight. She reached across the table and took his free hand.

"What difference does it make?"

"It matters to me."

His fingers curled around hers, and his thumb stroked the skin on the top of her index finger. She ignored the stirring of desire, but it was there, banked but burning brighter each time he touched her.

"Everybody over there in the sandbox talks about coming home. About the girl they left, about the family they left. I just wanted to stay there. Stay so far away that they could never get to me."

"The gang?"

"Yeah." Ty drew back his hands back and sat straight in his chair, both palms now flat on the table. His shoulders sagged and he looked like a man defeated. "I stayed away as long as I could, but Colt joined the service. Wanted to be like me. If I'd been here I could've stopped him."

Beth knew what had happened during Colt's tour of duty in Afghanistan. He had been taken prisoner and tortured and was the only survivor among his unit. Was that burden also on Ty's shoulders?

"Jake called me. Told me that Colt was in Walter Reed. They released him on the psych discharge. I picked them up in Phoenix. What a mess. He couldn't drive in the car. Stopped talking. Walked all the way from Phoenix to the rez. I helped him get situated in the mining cabin that belongs to my family."

"You came back to take care of your little brother."

"Yeah, that's about it." Ty put his hand on the top of his head and ruffled his hair. "But I made a mistake. Stopped by to see my dad down there in Phoenix. Couldn't resist."

"Why was that a mistake?" she asked.

He cast her a look filled with pain and she felt a stab of grief cut across her middle. Understanding struck.

Beth's eyes rounded. "You told him?"

"No, but he knows." Ty's answer was just above a whisper. "Figured it out. Just needed to see him behind bars and…" His words trailed off. He pushed his plate out of the way.

"He guessed."

Ty met her stare. "At first glance. Don't know how. But he knew. No one in the gang guessed."

"He can't get to you."

"I'm not worried about me. I'm worried about my mom because he knows the best way to hurt me is through her."

"He can't touch her from prison," Beth assured him.

"He's scheduled to be paroled."

Chapter Fifteen

Beth sat back in alarm. Ty's father would be paroled and his father knew that Faras had used his son to snatch the gang's leadership and his freedom. Ty was right to be worried. She needed to speak to Forrest about this. "When does he get out?"

"I don't know. Soon."

"I'll find out and I'll speak to Forrest about this. We'll come up with something to keep your family safe."

Ty heaved a heavy sigh. "Already lost Colt. He can't come back until you take down that Russian organization."

"We're making good progress on that. The Antelope Lake house where they held Ava Hood and Louisa Tah has yielded good evidence. We've identified all the men recovered and connected them to the Kuznetsov crime organization." She used the word *recovered* because all the men found at the temporary holding facility, where Ava Hood had been held, were all dead. They'd had a chance to capture Yury Churkin, a hired killer sent to murder Kee's fiancée,

Ava Hood. Unfortunately, Churkin had put a bullet through his brain before they got to him. Still, Churkin's presence on the rez had been connected to at least one death here, Dr. Richard Day, a FEMA physician. Now they needed to connect Churkin's actions to Usov's orders. The head of the southwestern region, Leonard Usov, was Beth's target. If she could implicate him, she'd have a chance to shut down the western arm of the surrogate ring.

They had only one suspect in custody, Anton Igoshin, the man who had fallen chasing Kacey Doka and broken his back. He was now a wheelchair user facing multiple charges, including kidnapping.

Ty laced his hands before him on the table.

"Faras wants me back in the gang. Seems I passed the test. He found his snitch and he requests me as his second." He lifted his chin. "Congratulations, Agent Hoosay. You've got your informer."

This was what she had wanted, wasn't it? The bureau finally had a man inside the Wolf Posse. Unfortunately, that man was Ty and she no longer saw him as just her informant. She'd read about agents who went undercover and got all mixed up with the people they worked with and lived with. They lost objectivity and began to see the people who trusted them as friends and confidants. She saw that happening to herself right now and did not know how to stop it. If she was honest with herself, she'd admit she had feelings for Ty. It hurt her to use him and endanger him.

"Maybe we can make my case, break the back of

the gang and make sure your father doesn't ever hurt your family again."

Ty's smug smile was back and he lolled back in his seat. "Great. How, exactly, do we do that?"

Now it was her turn to press a hand to her forehead. "I don't know. But we need to do all of it."

Ty stood and retrieved the dinner plates. "I helped Faras take power and in exchange he's left me out of the worst of the gang activities. But now that he's facing another power struggle, all that has changed." He carried the dishes to the sink and she cleared the rest of the table.

Beth knew Ty was smart, and his understanding of how things worked here was far better than hers. Informants provided information. But Beth had a real desire to include Ty in strategic planning.

"I think you could be more than an informant," she said, picking up a dish towel to dry the dishes he set in the strainer.

He quirked an eyebrow, mildly interested. "That so?"

"You have every reason to be suspicious. But you know as well as I do that if we remove Faras, whoever is challenging him will take over and things will soon be right back where they started."

"Chino Aria. He's the most likely challenger. Very territorial around Faras, but he's got some things going on that I'm not sure Faras condoned."

"What exactly?"

"I heard something from one of the newer recruits, Randy Tasa."

"The kid on the bike," said Beth.

Ty lowered his hands and turned to face her. "How do you know about him?"

"You were under surveillance. I saw you hassle him outside the roadhouse the night we met."

Ty shook the water and suds off his hands and shut off the tap. "Hassling? That what you saw?"

She felt the same doubt as when she had watched the interaction. It had occurred to her vaguely that Ty might be running him off.

"Randy is a smart kid with no father and a big sister already in the gang. He's got potential. Faras sees it and so do I. But Faras sees another member of the posse and I see a rabbit that might just escape the snare. I just gave him a shove in the right direction."

"They recruit kids that young?"

Randy was only fourteen.

"They do, but the interesting thing is that Faras didn't know Randy was working for him. Chino had him out there selling weed and Faras didn't know."

"So?" asked Beth.

"Faras used to know everything. Maybe the surrogate ring is taking all his attention or maybe Chino is working something on the side."

Beth leaned a hip against the counter and folded her arms beneath her breasts. "What do you think?"

"Chino is preparing a takeover. I'm sure."

"Because of one kid?"

Ty angled his head to the side and then righted it. The gesture reminded her of a shrug.

"If you are right we could work those two against each other," she said.

And just like that, they were talking strategy. Beth set up scenarios and Ty poked holes in them. They moved to the sofa, sat facing each other, each with a leg tucked up on the cushions. Beth scrawled notes on a pad on each member of the gang. Ty provided so much intelligence, it would have taken FBI months to get even close to this kind of inside information.

He also told her exactly why he had helped Faras recover Kacey Doka and the reason he'd done it.

"So you made a deal with Faras and so he reported to the Russians that the baby delivered by Zella Cole-lay had died?"

"Yes."

"Because Jake and his wife had decided to adopt that baby?"

"Zella escaped capture and delivered a baby. The Russians still wanted it because somewhere out there is a couple waiting for their biological offspring."

"Do the parents know? Do they understand where their surrogates come from?" asked Beth.

"I doubt it. But I don't know. All I know is that Faras found out that Zella's baby had arrived and sent two of the posse after her. I was watching Jake and when I saw that the ones that were after the infant were members of the Wolf Posse I knew they wouldn't stop, ever, unless I went to Faras."

"What did he say?"

"He agreed to report the infant deceased."

Beth was impressed. Ty had gotten Faras to give false information to his contacts.

Ty did not look smug over his coup. Instead he looked worried as he continued. "But Faras doesn't give something for nothing. He wanted my word that I'd start driving again. Up until then I just repaired the cars. Kept them moving faster than the competition and the authorities."

"Driving?"

"Pick-ups, escapes, deliveries."

"And he called and told you to pick up your younger brother's girlfriend, Kacey Doka."

"Exactly. I couldn't refuse without endangering Jake's baby."

"You could have come to the police."

Ty gave a mirthless laugh. "Right."

"Instead, you collected Kacey from in front of the clinic and drove her to her captors."

"Only after I called Colt and reported the drop location."

"Again, you could have called the police."

"Yes. And then I'd be dead. Kacey would be recaptured and Jake's new baby would be back with the Russians."

"You don't have very much confidence in us."

"We called the police on my father again and again. He went in and came back like a boomerang."

She understood his point. Without May's willingness to press charges, there was little to be done.

"You can't protect us," said Ty. "You guys come

in after a crime is committed. I was trying to keep the crimes from happening."

"You were trying to protect your family."

Ty looked away and she knew that she understood. He'd defended his brother's baby. He had told Colt where the drop was. And in telling her, he had just given Beth the information that could destroy him. She could use it to ensure his compliance, and she knew that she never would.

"You kept them all safe, Ty. But you have to let us help you or it won't stop. Sooner or later you'll fail or they'll figure out what you did."

"I know that. I was certain they'd figure it out after Kacey's escape. But Faras didn't hear what I did there to help her get clear of them, and the one survivor is in custody."

"Sequestered. He is out of general population for as long as it takes to close this case."

"What does that look like to you? A closed case?"

"We get the remaining girls back and shut down the operation, not just up here but all over the southwest. We make a case against Leonard Usov and possibly tie him to Kostya Kuznetsov in Atlanta."

"Who?"

"Usov runs all human trafficking operations here. He reports to the Kuznetsov crime family, and Kostya is their head."

"That's a big case."

"We have Betty Mills as a witness. The health care administrator made the calls to Faras. She's a treasure trove of information, but her attorney is smart. He

wants some concessions to ensure her full cooperation. Once she's on board, we arrest Faras and every
other member of the posse involved. Your tribal police has been outnumbered over two to one by this
gang. Not anymore. Once I have evidence, I get resources and we end this."

"We?" he asked.

"Yes, we." She took his hand and squeezed. The
gesture was intended to demonstrate they were a
team. Instead, something happened. Her breath
caught at the tingling awareness that blossomed over
her skin. Their eyes met and hunger surged as powerful as a waterfall. The hairs on her neck lifted and
her skin puckered. His breathing accelerated, making his nostrils flare.

"Ty?"

He was inching closer, his gaze now on her mouth.

Beth could have stopped him. She knew that just
a word, a gesture, and Ty would retreat. But she said
nothing because in her heart she wanted this. Her
soul yearned for the connection and her body ached
with need.

His mouth melted to hers, touching off a series of
tantalizing shocks that rippled over her skin and settled low in her belly. She did not know why her body
sang at his touch. It had been this way since she first
laid eyes on him. Back then she had thought him a
trickster. A man with two faces who showed her exactly what she wanted to see. She thought she knew
the truth of him. She thought a man as uncompli-

cated as Ty could be summed up in the contents of a manila folder.

He couldn't be. Ty was so much more.

His fingers grazed her neck, caressed her cheek and threaded into her hair. He tipped her back, trapping her between the sofa headrest and his hungry mouth. She reached for him with greedy fingers, dragging her nails up the skin of his back beneath his T-shirt. When she reached his shoulder blades, she tugged him against her. They fell together to the sofa, Ty on top. The weight of his chest against her torso was sweet torture. His hips pressed to hers and she raked her hands back down the long muscles beside his spine until she gripped him by the seat and rocked him forward.

Her tongue delved, dancing with his inner rhythmic thrusting that electrified her senses. She was surprised that it was Ty who halted their kiss. He lifted himself up on his forearms to peer down at her. He cast her a look of surprise and concern. "Do you know what you're doing?"

"I'm through with thinking for a while," she replied.

"Bad things happen when you stop thinking."

"And great things."

His smile was devilish. His dark eyes glittered. She brushed back the hair that fell forward over his forehead, her fingers gliding over the satin strand before tucking it behind his ear.

"I want to sleep with you, Ty."

"Have you thought about the consequences?"

"I'm on birth control and I have a feeling you have condoms close at hand."

"That's not the consequences I was talking about. As far as the Bureau is concerned, I'm your informant and you're undercover. I appreciate you wanting to appear to be my new girl, but I don't want you regretting this or getting into trouble because of something we do here."

"Break in professional ethics."

"Yup."

"Ty, it occurs to me that you don't often get what you want. You put your family's needs ahead of your own needs and even ahead of your own safety. You're a man who takes risks. I admire that."

"Tell me that if your boss finds out about this, you won't get fired."

She said nothing. At the very least she would receive a reprimand. Ty pulled away, sitting beside her hip on the sofa. She drew her legs from behind him and sat next to him a little too close.

"Only way they find out is if I tell them or you tell them," she said as he turned to meet her gaze and stared a long while. Then he stood and offered his hand.

Chapter Sixteen

She wasn't sure exactly how she got to the bedroom. All she knew for certain was that she had hopped out of her boots, dragged off her socks and shed her slacks, all while kissing Ty. She had removed her personal weapon and holster, which had been clipped to her belt, before stepping from her slacks. Hemi had risen from her dog bed to follow them and Ty had issued a command to stay that had sent his dog back to the living room. Then Ty had carried her, half-dressed, to his bed. She had set her holstered weapon and badge on his bedside table beside her handcuffs. Then she had torn his shirt over his head as he slipped her panties over her thighs.

The danger and the need mingled within her. She knew it was a misstep and that the consequences could be enormous. But some part of her didn't care. Having Ty was worth it all. When he stretched her out on his bed, they were naked. Nothing shielded her from the luscious slide of his heated flesh on hers. His rough calloused hands stroked her, each touch feeding her desire.

"I need you," he said.

She lifted her feet to the bed and splayed her thighs. Ty's eyes widened and his expression turned hungry. His mouth descended to her earlobe, sucking and nipping her sensitive flesh as he descended from her neck to the blade of her collarbone and below.

They came together in a rush of need and madness. He laced his fingers through hers and trapped her hands beside her head. Ty gazed down at her with dark soulful eyes, his expression one of pleasure marred by pain. She watched him move as she felt the velvety glide of his body connecting with hers. Perfection, she thought. Just as she'd known it would be.

And then the whirlwind of sensation took her. She gasped and lifted herself at the pleasure arcing her spine. His mouth found hers and he followed her a moment later. He held her as the bliss rolled through her. The pleasure was bone-deep and raw. She closed her eyes, knowing that this was the man she had always dreamed of and he had appeared in her life in the worst form imaginable. She knew there would be regret and that this relationship was doomed from the start. But she had started it and she was not sorry. Time enough for regrets tomorrow. Tonight she would hold him in her arms and pretend that she could keep this man who had so unexpectedly crept into her heart.

Ty fell beside her on the mattress, panting. He rolled to his side and gathered her close as the sweat glistened on their spent bodies. Gradually, their breathing came back to normal and their skin dried.

She snuggled close, trying to escape the chilly air that disturbed her doze. Tendrils of cold air wafted through his bedroom from the open window beside the bedside table. Beth shivered. Ty roused enough to draw her closer.

She fought the cold, not the cold of the room but the one creeping back inside her. This time with Ty was right—so right and so good. It made her wonder what they could be like together and how they could make that happen. But to have him she'd have to give up her dream or take him from his family. It was impossible, but her mind would not give up and continued to throw what-ifs at her as her heart ached with need.

Ty peered at her.

"Cold?" he asked, his voice lethargic and deep.

"Mmm," she murmured, and inclined her head.

He tugged the bedding from beneath them and slipped them under the blankets. They nestled together, her forehead on his cheek, his arm about her shoulder, her hand over his heart.

He toyed with her curly hair, winding a strand around his index finger.

"Beth, I know the scent of your hair—" he inhaled "—is orchids and I know the soft feel of your body." He stroked his palm up her ribs. "But you haven't told me anything about yourself except the bullet points of your resume."

She stiffened and his hand slipped away.

"What do you want to know?" she asked, feeling the walls rising around her.

"Everything."

She said nothing as she struggled against the need to unlock her past to him. It wasn't professional, so why did she have to fight to keep silent?

"Anything," he whispered.

The silence stretched and the tension in her mounted.

He nuzzled her head with his cheek. "You were wearing a rodeo buckle the night I first saw you. Was that yours or part of your cover?"

She could not help smiling at the memories. "Both. I used to ride when I was a teenager. My mother allowed me to compete because horses are so closely tied to our culture."

"You must have been good."

Back then barrel racing was an acceptable risk. One that her mother allowed, and there were few enough of those. Beth was not even permitted to ride in a friend's car in high school. The smothering sensation returned to her. "That buckle was for barrel racing at our annual rodeo."

Her answer must have encouraged him because he asked another more personal question. "Did you grow up on the reservation up there in Oklahoma?"

"I lived there when I was young. Registered member. They dropped the blood quota a while ago, so if your parent is a member, you're eligible. My dad didn't like Oklahoma because it's so cold and rural on the rez. He missed Miami. But my mom's family was there." She stopped talking because she already felt she'd said too much.

Ty lifted himself up on an elbow to stare at her. "He was?"

"My father is from the Caribbean. So I'm brown, but not the same sort of brown as most of the kids there." She tugged at a tight curl in emphasis.

"So you felt different."

"Yeah. The kids were okay. The rez was okay, too, but…" She threw up a hand. "It made my dad unhappy to be there. It was like he couldn't wait to get back to the army and away from us."

"You blame your mom for that?" he asked.

"She could have gone with him instead of making a life without him there."

"What did she do there on the rez?"

"She's a neurosurgeon."

Ty's eyebrows lifted; he was clearly impressed. "Really?"

She nodded. "Anyway, they met when he was stationed there and they might have loved each other but not enough for him to stay or her to go." She hated talking about this next part and counseled herself not to cry. "My dad was an army ranger, but he died when I was thirteen."

"KIA?" asked Ty, meaning "killed in action."

"No. Traffic accident. He was riding his motorcycle and was hit by the driver of a pickup truck who never saw him. The impact threw him from the bike and he was hit again by a car traveling in the opposite direction. He died of his injuries at the scene." She got the whole thing out and only then did her throat close up. She made an involuntary high whining sound.

Ty gathered her in his arms.

"I'm so sorry, Beth." He held her and rubbed her back as she struggled with her tears. "I'm surprised you ride."

"He used to take me with him on his bike. After he died I missed it. Riding is like being with him. My mom flipped when she found out, of course. She always called people who ride bikes 'organ donors.' Then my dad died and he actually was one. She doesn't say that anymore. When I came home with my first bike, a Suzuki, she ordered me to sell it. But I wouldn't. My act of defiance, I suppose. I was so mad at her after Dad died. It was like she caused it. I know that sounds crazy. I know it's not fair or even rational, but it's how I felt. If we'd gone with him, he wouldn't have been on that bike in Oklahoma. Anyway, I'm glad I kept riding, because I love my bike."

"I understand that. Did you join the service because of him?"

"Yes. And the Bureau. Dad had been accepted…" She hesitated and took two deep breaths, then plunged back in. "Before the accident, he joined the FBI. It was his next move after the army. Got his dream placement, too, in DC."

And that placement would have taken him away from them permanently.

Ty's eyes rounded and his expression went wary. He wasn't stupid. But she wasn't doing this for her father. She wanted to make a difference, too. Was that so wrong? Her mother thought so. It was why Beth stopped calling home.

"But I also joined…" She shook her head, still not believing she'd told him about her father or that she was even considering bringing up her mom.

"Also joined…" he coaxed.

She'd had enough. Her stomach ached from talking about this and she needed an antacid.

"So," he said, "you'll sleep with me. But you won't tell me the other reason why you joined the army?"

She could feel him drawing away. It made her mad, too, his withdrawal, because she wouldn't give him what he wanted.

"I joined to get away from her." She spat the words.

His face registered surprise, but he didn't speak.

She blew out a breath and reined in her anger. "After he died, my mom got weird. She drove me everywhere and wouldn't let me in anyone's car but hers. I was going crazy."

"Protecting you." Ty's voice was just above a whisper as if he understood and was taking her side.

Beth doubled down, getting it all out. "Suffocating me. After he died she forbade me to ride horses. I wasn't allowed to play soccer. She said that was too dangerous because of the possibility of head injuries. So when I turned eighteen, I bought a bike. I knew she'd go crazy. That's exactly why I bought it. And she did. Ultimatums, the whole thing. I joined the army to get away from her, but I stayed because I fit there. They promote you on merit. You succeed or fail because of what you do, not who your parents might be or if you look a certain way."

"I remember," he said. "No history or past mistakes, just what they can see."

"The Bureau is different but also the same. You rise based on what you produce, what convictions you make. Merit, like in the army. They don't have many agents who look like me. The demographics are still mostly men and mostly white. I'm different there in a good way. It makes me stand out and it got me this assignment."

"Your mom still in Oklahoma?"

"Yes. She lives and works in the city and keeps a place on the rez."

"And you took this case because you could help our people," said Ty.

She hadn't. They'd picked her because the database said she was Apache and she'd been happy to let that distinction help her along.

She lifted her gaze to meet his and felt small as she admitted the truth. "I took the assignment to make a big case."

"Why is that so important?"

She didn't know how to explain it or if she really wanted to explain it.

"Because I can make more of a difference in a bigger field office," she said.

"Oklahoma is not a small place," he reminded her.

"I hate Oklahoma."

"Because your dad hated it."

She dropped her gaze. "The best agents are in New York and DC."

"Ambition, then. I understand that."

But he didn't approve. She could tell by the way he rolled to his back and folded his uninjured arm behind his head to stare up at the ceiling.

"I was ambitious once," he said. "Then I realized that I was one small fish in a big ocean. You know what little fish do, right?" He turned to her.

"What?" she asked.

"They try to stay alive."

She made a sound in her throat that acknowledged the truth in that. Then she curled against him. He didn't stop her, but neither did he take her in his arms again. There was a barrier rising between them again.

"Big world. I can't save it. But I try to save the ones I can."

Their goals were different. Was he thinking that she didn't need him or wouldn't need him for long? He planned to stay here with his family and she was leaving as soon as they let her. She wanted to take back what she'd told him. Take it all back. She had position and authority already. But he had something more valuable, he had people he cared about and who cared about him, real living people, while she was still trying to make her father proud.

She fell asleep to the rhythm of their heartbeats.

The ringing of Beth's phone woke her from a deep sleep. She glanced at the phone's display and saw it was three in the morning and that the call was from her supervisor, Agent Luke Forrest.

"Hoosay here."

"Get to the tribal police station," said Forrest.

"Mills committed suicide tonight and someone set the clinic on fire."

Beth threw herself to a seated position. Beside her, Ty sat up against the headboard, his body a dark silhouette in the bedroom. It had come too soon, the crash of reality that ripped her from his embrace.

The records! The Bureau had removed what they deemed significant, but there was always the chance they could unearth more.

"How bad is the fire?"

"Bad enough."

"Maybe kids. A Halloween prank?" she asked.

"Started in the records room. When the firefighters are done, we'll sort through what's left. Meet me there."

"En route," said Beth, but Forrest had already hung up. She slipped from the bed. "I have to go."

He captured her wrist. "It's a trap."

She hesitated. He wore no shirt and she could clearly see the stitches that ran across his shoulder, the wound he had suffered at Antelope Lake. Why hadn't she remembered that during their lovemaking? They could have torn the stitches. "What?"

"It's just like the nonexistent meth lab on Canyon Ridge Road. Set a fire and see who shows up. My girlfriend shouldn't be there. I know that much."

She mulled it over. What he said was smart. "I'll be careful. But I have to go."

Ty released her wrist and she snatched her pistol and badge from the bedside table. She recovered her underthings on the way to the living room, gathering her slacks and shirt along the way. She sat on the couch and flicked on a side lamp to draw on her ankle-high boots. Hemi came out to keep her company.

Ty stepped into the hall a moment later, leaning against the wall. He now wore a pair of gym shorts and nothing else. The red scars on his shoulder marred the perfection of his skin. His arms and face were tanned, a workingman's tan, she realized.

"Beth, you're undercover. Here with me."

"They won't see me at the fire."

"What if they see you leaving here right now?"

She glanced toward the windows and the darkness looming all around them. Then she gathered her courage. "It's my job."

"What am I supposed to do?"

She cast him an impatient look. Hemi moved to stand by the door, glancing back at them.

"Everything you do doesn't have to involve risk."

He was psychoanalyzing her based on a five-minute conversation that they never should have had. She stood and grabbed an antacid, popping it into her mouth.

"Stay here and wait for me to come back."

She holstered her weapon and looped the lanyard over her neck. She couldn't stay. This was her case, her chance.

He snorted and his chin dipped. "Yeah, right. Play time's over and you're back on the clock."

He turned and retreated toward the bedroom, snapping his fingers to call his dog. Hemi trotted after him. She stood and considered going after him. But what could she say? She did have a job to do and it did matter what they had shared but not enough to change anything. As she had feared. Ty was the man she wanted and could not have, at least not for long.

Beth shrugged into her leather jacket and retrieved her motorcycle helmet on her way out the door.

TY HAD GONE back to bed, but he didn't sleep. Instead he lay on his back with his arm across his forehead and watched the light rise until he could see all the objects in the room, including the pair of handcuffs she had left behind on his bedside table. She'd been gone for hours. Was she safe? Did she need him? Ty threw back the covers and sat on the edge of his bed.

Hemi groaned and lifted her head. She had slept on the dog bed she must have dragged in here some-time in the night. Usually he brought her dog bed into this room at night, but she could do it herself and he had been distracted.

She came to sit beside him, resting her enormous head on his thigh while staring up at him with soul-ful eyes. He stroked the thick fur on her ruff with distraction. Hemi sighed. When his hand stilled, she stretched and walked to the door, her toenails clicking on the wood floor. She paused in the doorway, look-ing back at him as if asking if he was coming along.

"Need to go out, girl?"

Hemi's reaction—hurrying toward the front door as she wagged her tail—was answer enough. Ty let her out and then retreated to the bathroom. He was half-dressed and shaving when his cell phone rang.

He snatched it up, hoping it was Beth. His shoulders sagged as he realized it was Faras calling at 6:05 a.m.

"Not good."

Chapter Seventeen

When Faras called, you didn't ask him why. Ty fed
Hemi and took her along, fixing the carrier to the
back of his Harley. He reached the clubhouse, as Faras
called the Wolf Posse's headquarters.

Ty was surprised to be greeted by Chino, an unlikely guard, at the entrance to the property. Ordinar-
ily, his second in command would not be given the
menial task of sitting in his automobile and checking
in arrivals. Something was going on.

Chino cast him a glare and waved him on. Ty was
happy for the roaring engine of his motorcycle, which
made speech between them difficult. He rolled up
to the ranch property, noticing again the number of
new trucks. Once upon a time he was all that kept
the posse's old fleet of battered high-mileage vehicles moving. That time had come and gone, and Ty's
usefulness dwindled as the number of autos under
warranty grew.

Ty released Hemi from the crate and they were
ushered in by the guard at the door. Once inside,
he found Faras sitting alone at a large dining room

table. Before him was his open laptop, a cigarette smoldering in an ashtray and, at his elbow, a full cup of coffee.

Faras pinned his weary gaze on Ty.

"About time," he grumbled. Then he lifted his cigarette and took a long drag, exhaling smoke toward the ceiling, where it swirled, forming a blue-gray haze.

Ty pointed to the couch, and Hemi hopped to the cushions, stretching out for a nap. Ty continued through the living room to stand before Faras on the opposite side of the rectangular table.

"What's up?" asked Ty.

"You see Chino outside?"

Ty inclined his head and glanced toward the door. The house was uncharacteristically empty. Some of that could be blamed on the earliness of the hour. But Faras usually had a guard inside the premises.

"Found out the Russians called him. Believe that?"

"Who? Chino?"

Faras took a drag on the cigarette and nodded.

"What does that mean?"

"It means he's trying to take over. Doing an end-run. He knows that Usov is ticked at me. Knows Quinton narced on me and that the guys are getting restless because tribal arrested Hauser and Mills. Perfect timing. Remember when I took over?"

"That was different. The posse had lost its leader."

"Yeah, but I was a long shot. Only reason I'm sitting here is you, bro. Don't think I forget it, either."

Ty wondered if Faras was appreciative enough to

let him go free and clear. But he knew Faras well enough to understand that he had not called Ty to his side at this hour to release him from his obligation or to offer thanks. Faras had helped him entrap his father. Ty had owed him, though that debt should now be more than paid.

"I want you here full-time starting right now," said Faras.

That was definitely not going to work. Ty drew up a chair and sat down. He folded his open hands before him on the top of the table, partly to show he was getting down to business, but also to show Faras where his hands were.

"I just don't know who to trust. Time to fall back on the ones who were there from the start. You know?" asked Faras.

"Yeah. Understandable. So the Russians… How's that going to work with Dr. Hauser dead and the clinic closed?" Ty did not mention that the clinic had been set on fire, but wondered if Faras might already know.

"They don't need the clinic or Hauser. They just want the posse to pick up candidates."

Ty had never asked how this part of the operation worked. Up until three weeks ago, when Kacey Doka arrived after escaping captivity by the Russians, he didn't even know it was happening. But it was like driving by a horrific accident. You couldn't unsee that.

"How does that happen, exactly?" asked Ty.

"I used to pick rejects from our recruitment. Girls we didn't want because they were too messed up or their families were. Easy to find the ones that no one would miss. But now tribal police are on to us and they're going to take note of every girl who 'runs away.'" Faras used air quotes around the words *runs away*.

"So what are you going to do?"

"I don't know, man. This is bad. I have to deliver four girls, so I got bigger problems than Chino trying to take the reins."

Ty thumped his hands on the table. "Hate to add to your troubles, but my dad will be out soon."

Faras took another long drag on his cigarette, then stubbed it out. He lifted his coffee mug and took a sip. For a moment Ty thought Faras was weighing his options or brainstorming a plan. But then he slammed his laptop shut, leaving his hands splayed upon the black plastic casing as he glared at Ty. "You take care of him. You hear? This time you do like I said and kill the bastard."

Ty understood. Faras would be of no help where his dad was concerned. Ty was on his own on that one.

But by ordering him to take care of his father, Faras had presented him with the opportunity to escape Faras's demand to move in permanently.

"All right. I'll take care of it."

Ty stood and exited the Wolf Posse's headquarters. Hemi roused as Ty strode through the living room and hopped down from the couch to fall in step beside him as he cleared the front door.

He almost made it out, but Faras called after him.

"I was thinking of taking girls that are passing through. You know?" He drew out a new cigarette from the pack and lit it. The tip flared orange for the intake of his breath. "Take them from outside the boundaries of the rez or take them at drinking parties. We always get outsiders at parties."

"Outsiders?" Ty asked. Faras was getting desperate.

"Yeah. You know, any women from outside the rez?" Faras set the cigarette in the ashtray and quirked an eyebrow. "I just need four more and those bastards will move on and I'll be back to business as usual."

Which meant drug sales, protection and money laundering. Ty had never seen Faras look so frazzled. If he didn't know what Faras had done and what he was capable of doing, he'd almost feel sorry for him. But Ty knew that a cornered animal was the most dangerous sort.

Faras drew out a cigarette from the pack on the table and then realized he had one smoldering in the ashtray. He slipped the tube of tobacco back into the pack and turned his attention on Ty. "You know any women who don't belong here?"

Did he mean Beth? Did he actually think he'd turn over his girlfriend? Or did Faras know who and what Beth really was? He schooled himself to hold a blank expression.

"No," said Ty.

Faras slipped the open pack of cigarettes back into his shirt pocket. "Think about it, bro. You ain't known her that long. Then it'd be one down and three to go."

Ty's jaw tightened.

Faras's smile was cold as winter frost. "You take care of this trouble with your dad. Permanently. Then get back here. If he ain't out yet, come back. I need four girls in their hands by Friday or Chino won't have to challenge me."

Ty headed out with Hemi trailing beside him. His canine needed no assistance in hopping up to her traveling crate and sat with tongue lolling as he fixed the harness about her. He needed to find Beth and warn her that she was on the capture list.

Ty stopped at the top of the drive for the rolling gate to open and permit his exit. Chino made him wait. Finally, the barrier rolled back and Chino flipped him the bird as he roared away on his sled. He made sure he was out of sight and earshot before pulling over. His cell phone offered him no service. Ty swore. Hemi rested her large chin upon his shoulder. He lifted his hand to give her an absent scratch on the cheek. Then they were off again, heading for Piñon Forks.

He was careful to park at the clinic because he couldn't very well pull in to the parking lot of tribal headquarters. His bike was too distinctive to be seen right in front of the building that housed the police station. Luckily, the tribe's clinic was a separate building and his big brother worked there, giving him all the reason he needed to visit. Plus, Beth might be here because of the fire.

He saw none of the posse's vehicles as he pulled in. It didn't mean they were not here.

Despite the damage to the reception area and medical records, the clinic was open. Ty entered through the main doors to find the waiting room half-full. A desk and computer had been set up in the waiting area before a blue plastic tarp that covered the fire-damaged section beyond. The burned smell permeated the chilly air despite the fan set to high in the open window.

Ty asked the new receptionist if he could speak to his brother. Kee appeared a few minutes later. Ty explained that he wanted Kee to take him through the clinic and out the back door, where he could cross between the buildings and into tribal headquarters.

They walked side by side past the exam rooms and into the women's health clinic in the back of the building.

"Any word on Dad?" asked Kee.

"Not yet."

Kee grimaced. "Maybe I should go out and see Mom after work today."

Ty left him at the back door and headed for the station, where he met with Officer Wetselline, who was manning the squad room with Kee's fiancé, Ava Hood, the former Yavapai detective turned dispatcher.

Ava used the radio to call Wallace Tinnin, their police chief, who was at home this morning. Ty waited in his office for the five minutes it took the chief to drive from his home to headquarters. Once Tinnin was in his office, Ty relayed everything that Faras had told him.

"Be too much to ask, I suppose, to have Chino and Faras kill each other in a power struggle," said Tinnin.

"Any word from the prison on when my father will be released?"

"Not yet. Paperwork is pending." Tinnin offered Ty some coffee, but he declined.

"Beth is not answering her phone. Can you get word to her?"

"I'll sure give it my best shot."

He was referring to Luke Forrest, the agent in charge of the Russian trafficking case.

"You get cell-phone service out at your place?" asked the chief.

"Sure do."

"So go home and I'll call when I make contact."

Ty did as he was told and spent the rest of a very restless day working on replacing the head gasket on the '76 Cadillac Eldorado and waiting for Beth to return or Tinnin to get word from his…what? Girlfriend? Supervisor? FBI contact? He was her informer and despite the night they had spent together, Beth had not included him in her plans. Ty had a good long time to think about the limitations of their arrangement, and the fact that just because he wanted something did not mean he would have it. His life had been full of many such dreams brought to dust by the heel of reality. He knew who he was and what he was. He had just forgotten for a moment.

On the bright side, the Eldorado was now running and, man, that engine purred.

When his phone rang at four that afternoon, he snatched it from his pocket on the first ring. The display announced that the phone call was from Kee.

"Hey, Kee. What's up?" asked Ty.

"Abbie is missing."

Chapter Eighteen

Ty straightened as his entire body flashed hot and cold. He swallowed, wondering if Faras would have dared to snatch his little sister.

Beth and Abbie. That would leave him only two more girls needed. This was why Ty didn't own a gun. He knew the limits of his temper, and his marines training ensured that he was a deadly shot.

"Repeat that," he said.

Kee did and Ty felt his world tilting off its axis. He didn't know how or why, but he was certain that this was his fault.

Kee gave him the details. Abbie had been taken from their yard twenty minutes earlier. The police were there. Winnie Doka, one of the three girls fostering with his mother, had witnessed the abduction. But they hadn't taken Winnie. To Ty that meant the attack was specific—his sister, and just his sister.

"She said the guy was big, bald."

Chino, Ty thought. "What color was he?"

"Brown. She thinks he was Apache."

"I'm on my way." But first he would speak to

Faras. He knew Faras would tell him nothing on the phone. He'd need to show up in person at the Wolf Posse headquarters if he had any hope of getting answers. He left Hemi at the garage and called Beth again before departing. His call was flipped over to voice mail. This time he left a message.

Why would Faras take Abbie? Or had Chino acted on his own? Was it possible that Abbie's abduction was unrelated to the Russian surrogate ring?

He roared down the road to the Wolf Posse's crib and slowed only long enough for the gate to gape enough to permit his Harley.

Faras met him on the front step.

"She's not here," he said, hands raised.

But he knew she was missing. Ty rolled the bike onto its kickstand and dismounted.

"You have her?" asked Ty.

"Insurance. Your new girl, she isn't a drifter. Is she? She's a narc. So you got a decision to make. Either she dies or your sister does."

The rage poured through Ty and he took a step toward Faras. Chino lifted a double-barreled shotgun with a smile.

"Go for it," he challenged.

"Beth or Abbie," repeated Faras. "You pick."

Ty forced himself to breathe past the panic swirling with the rage.

"What do you want, exactly?" he asked.

"I'm sending you to settle up with the Russians, get our final payout and make the last delivery. You need four women. Get them any way you like. Take your narc as one, but one way or another, she disappears. Meanwhile, I hold your sister safe and sound until I hear from Usov that you've made the drop."

"How am I supposed to deliver four women?"

"Apply yourself." Faras glared. "Drop is tomorrow." He tossed a piece of paper at him. "There's the address. Four girls including your narc girlfriend. You could take those kids fostering with your mom. Three of them, right?"

There were. Jackie, Winnie and Shirley Doka, Kacey's sisters. Shirley was eleven. Ty felt something in his middle harden to glass. Had he really once counted Faras as a friend?

"They expect you in a single auto. Take the Caddy you're working on. That one has a four-body trunk."

Ty turned to go, but Faras issued a last warning.

"If I hear you are looking for Abbie, I'll be so disappointed and something bad will happen."

For the first time, Ty wondered if he had made the right choice by helping Faras take over the Wolf Posse. Ty's father was vicious and volatile. But he did not have Faras's capacity for manipulation. His father used his fists to keep order. Faras used the ones you loved.

Ty paused and then spoke over his shoulder. "Understood."

He left Faras and drove toward Koun'nde. Long ago, he had handled his father without telling anyone in his family what he had done. They all thought that it was just good luck and his bad driving that had finally eliminated the dangerous tyrant from their midst. Ty didn't believe in luck. But despite his attempts to keep his family safe, Colt was in witness protection, Kee and Jake had almost been killed by members of the Wolf Posse and Russian mob and his sister was now a captive.

Ty's back was to the wall. For far too long he had walked the fine line between the posse and the law. He was sick of it. Sick of trying to find opportunities to undermine the posse while still protecting his family and keeping himself out of the morgue. He was sure it had not been Faras's intention, but in taking his little sister, he had flipped some switch inside Ty. He was no longer an ally or an attack dog or a turncoat, snitch or bystander. He was in this, and Faras was the enemy.

Ty would not stop until he had his sister back and had destroyed every last member of this gang.

His first call was to Jake and his second was to Detective Jack Bear Den. They were meeting him at his mother's house in Koun'nde. Beth and her FBI supervisor could catch up when they became available. He wasn't waiting.

He had twenty-four hours to destroy the Wolf Posse, capture the Russians and get his sister back.

Jake was already there when Ty arrived and he had a police unit stationed across the end of the drive. Officer Wetselline moved to allow Ty access. Bear Den arrived shortly afterward. Jake had called Kee, who had uncharacteristically left the tribe's health care clinic with Jake's wife, Lori, in charge. Kee started talking to Ty before the dust from Ty's bike had even settled.

The men gathered in the circular dirt driveway in front of his mother's home. Ty rocked his bike to the kickstand.

Having four boys raised here in this modest home meant that May Redhorse had given up having a front yard years ago in favor of extra parking for her sons' trucks, so there was plenty of room for the extra vehicles.

"We need the help of Tribal Thunder," said Jake.

Tribal Thunder was the warrior sect of their medicine society, the elite group Ty had once foolishly wished to be asked to join. Stupid to think such a group would ever want him. But today, he sure needed them. Tribal Thunder was called into action whenever there was a threat to the tribe. They had protected Kacey Doka for a time after she escaped her captors. Ty knew that both Jake's wife, Lori, and Jake were members of this elite band of protectors. Their entry only made his shortfall more painful.

Kee interjected his opinion. "I'd call Kenshaw. He has connections outside the tribe."

Jake said, "Kenshaw has been working with the FBI on the dam collapse. He is the only one who managed to infiltrate the eco-extremists' operation, and his cover has never been blown."

Bear Den scowled, thrusting his fists onto his hips as he narrowed his eyes at Jake. Ty got the feeling that this information was classified.

Jake faced Bear Den. "She's my sister, Jack."

Bear Den's hands dropped to his sides and he nodded, then faced Ty. "Jake's right. Kenshaw has connections all over the state. I agree to bringing him in. But we must also involve the FBI. The chief is getting to both Forrest and Hoosay."

Ty's mouth twitched and his stomach squeezed in irritation. "Beth got a call last night about the fire and I haven't been able to get a hold of her since."

Kee took that one. "The fire at the health care clinic damaged our medical records. We suspect it was a clumsy attempt to destroy evidence. Our firefighters made short work of the blaze. It will take a while to sort through the soggy mass of paperwork."

"There's good reason to suspect that the paper records will not jibe with what Betty Mills entered into the computer system," said Bear Den.

"Why weren't they removed already?"

Bear Den shrugged. "Oversight."

"And Betty's dead?" asked Ty.

"Suicide," said Bear Den. "Tore up her skirt for a noose."

Ty shook his head as he pictured Betty swinging from her designer skirt in her cell.

"You didn't have her on suicide watch?" asked Ty.

"No, we did not," answered Bear Den. "Because she was working with us, filling in the pieces. The FBI was building a case against the Russians, and Betty was hopeful because her attorney was working on a deal to arrange a reduced sentence and preferential placement. But something happened, because her death and the clinic's fire on the same night is just too much of a coincidence for my liking."

"What?" asked Jake.

"You ask me," said Ty, "someone got to her. Yesterday she had one visitor, her youngest boy, Clinton."

Boy was a stretch, thought Ty, as Clinton was in his midtwenties.

"Until yesterday not one of her three sons would see her. She had no visits from them or their children. But then Clinton shows up and his mother kills herself the same day."

Kee scratched his chin. Jake rested a hand on the grip of his service weapon, and Ty spoke up.

"Someone threatened her family," said Ty. "Clinton came to tell her they were in danger."

Bear Den met his gaze and Ty thought he saw respect in the big man's expression.

"My thoughts exactly. Now we have no witness."

"Wolf Posse or the Russians?" asked Ty.

Jack shook his head. "Not sure. FBI is questioning Clinton now."

"Great. But how are we getting Abbie back?" asked Kee.

Bear Den's and Jake's radios both came alive in unison as Officer Wetselline called from the end of the drive.

"I've got Agents Forrest and Hoosay here."

"Let them up," said Bear Den.

"Tinnin is coming in behind them," said Wetselline.

His car moved from the driveway entrance and a

black Escalade rolled past. Behind him, slowing down to make the turn, was Tinnin's official SUV. The stencil on the back fender was the tribal seal. The front door panel carried the police emblem and the word *Chief* below in bold black letters. The police chief drove all the way up to the gathering and opened his door, swinging himself around to face them. His leg, broken in the dam collapse last month, was now in a black plastic boot that made walking awkward, but he was finally done with the crutches.

Bear Den caught them up.

"Seems we have two operations," said Agent Forrest when Bear Den had finished. "Ty needs to make contact with the Russians tomorrow and simultaneously extract Abigail Redhorse from her captors in the Wolf Posse."

"The Russians are expecting Ty," said Tinnin.

"Anyone else shows up and we lose the possibility of locating our missing women and we lose Abbie," said Jake.

"We need to find Abbie," said Ty.

"And the missing," said Beth.

"I want Leonard Usov," said Forrest.

"You look a lot like Ty," said Tinnin to Jake.

Ty and Jake looked at each other. Jake's hair reached past his shoulders and he wore it back with a black elastic tie threaded with red cloth, while Ty clipped his hair chin-length and wore it loose. Jake's mouth often tipped down and Ty's naturally lifted up at the corners, making it seem as if he was perpetually up to something. But their facial features were very similar, their eyes a near match and their builds close enough to be, well, brothers.

"Yeah?" said Ty, inviting Tinnin to continue with a motion of his hand.

"So we need Ty in two places," said Tinnin. "He needs to make contact with the Russians. But honestly I would much rather have a police officer there to make that contact. And we need him to get past the Wolf Posse members who are likely holding his sister."

"You want Jake to pretend to be me?" asked Ty.

"Yes. And I want you to bluff your way past the posse to get to Abbie."

"Don't we have to find her first?" asked Bear Den.

"I'll take the kidnapping operation," said Beth, calling dibs on Abbie's abduction case and Ty all in one.

"I'll oversee the operation to make contact with the Russians," said Agent Forrest.

"What about the women? The Russians will be expecting me to be transporting four women, one of which is supposed to be Beth," Ty reminded them.

"Well, they are just doomed to disappointment."

Tinnin looked at Ty. "You know every member of the Wolf Posse."

Ty inclined his head.

"So find out where they are, each one, because one or more of them has your sister."

"I'm supposed to be kidnapping women."

"Jake and I will handle that. You find your sister, and when you have her, you call me so I can arrest Faras." Forrest glanced at the paper Ty held. "What's that?"

"Address of the meet," said Ty.

Tinnin held out his hand. Ty extended the page and Beth clasped his wrist, bringing his hand between them.

"If he does this," Beth interjected, "he does so in exchange for both the Bureau and tribal dropping any and all pending charges against him."

All the men stared at her. Forrest and Bear Den glared. Jake gaped and Tinnin smiled. Was she really negotiating an agreement for him?

"Tribal will take that deal," said Tinnin.

All gazes turned to Forrest. Beth had made a play that clearly annoyed her supervisor. He was the one who could put forth her name for promotion. The way he was staring daggers at her, Ty realized the chance of that ever happening had just gone up in flames and she'd done that for him. Why would she do that?

"What are you doing?" he whispered.

"Just wait," she replied out of the side of her mouth.

"Whose side are you on, Agent Hoosay?" asked Bear Den.

"Ty's," she answered.

Forrest tucked his chin and glared at Beth. Ty held his breath. What had she done? Beth had publicly advocated for him in a time when Forrest needed the information he held in his hand.

Forrest spat his answer. "Done."

"He gets the deal in writing today," she said.

Forrest nodded and motioned for the information with an impatient hand. Ty handed over the address.

Bear Den lifted his chin toward Ty. "Faras underestimated you. Never figured you'd come to us."

"Don't make me sorry," said Ty.

Jake pulled the elastic tie from his long hair. "Looks like I need a haircut." He turned toward the house, and shouted, "Ma!"

Ty smiled. Their mother had given them each their haircuts throughout their childhood, beginning with bangs and shoulder-length clips. Only Kee, who preferred short hair, went elsewhere for his grooming. Ty, Jake and even Colt, until he had left, all continued to have their mother cut their hair. If anyone could replicate Ty's style, it was their mom.

"What about Colt?" Ty asked Forrest.

"You lost me," said the agent.

"If you get him—Usov, I mean—can Colt and Kacey come home?"

Tinnin inhaled and glanced toward the sky, as he processed the question and implications. Finally he met Ty's gaze. "If that's what they want. But Colt is doing well where he is. He and Kacey are both working and Colt sees a counselor about the trauma he endured and his PTSD. He's talking now."

"He can do all that here," said Ty.

"Yes. But it is up to them. You'd understand if after being abducted by a member of her tribe and held captive for months, Kacey was not anxious to come home."

"I'd disagree," said Kee. "I saw her leaving her brothers and sisters. She wants to come home."

"All right. First things first. Okay?" said Forrest.

Yes, thought Ty. First he'd find his baby sister while Jake helped the Feds close down the Russian surrogate ring. Then they'd get their little brother to come home.

He shook his head at the chances of all that going right. Worry pressed down on him. His head began a dull ache at his temples.

Jake appeared on the front porch carrying a battered kitchen chair. May appeared behind him, a comb and her sewing scissors in her hand. This pair of shears was used solely for fabric and hair and woe to any of her children caught using them for any other purpose.

Jake sat and May pulled the elastic from his hair. Jake's expression was stoic and May's pained. She combed out the strands until they sat across Jake's back in perfect order. Then came the snip of the scissors.

Chapter Nineteen

Beth sucked the last antacid in the pack, the minty flavor ruined by the taste of chalk, as Ty drove them in Jake's Silver F-150 pickup back from Turquoise Ridge. They'd been up all night checking each member of the posse. Ty now wore Jake's clothing and his hair was tugged back in an elastic band, smoothed with hair gel to keep the short strands in place. The red cloth tie hid most of the evidence that his hair was nowhere near as long as Jake's had been.

It hadn't taken him long to figure out what she had done.

"You came here to make a big case," he said.

Her stomach tightened as she anticipated where this conversation might lead.

"Yet you chose to look for my sister, a simple kidnapping, instead of overseeing Jake's contact with the Russian mob."

"This operation might lead to the apprehension of Faras Pike." Her throat was also coated with chalk and she had to clear it to continue. "And furnish necessary information to tie this gang to the Russian crime organization."

"Yeah, yeah. It will get you assigned back to your desk in Oklahoma."

His skin glowed blue in the turquoise light from the truck's dashboard. "Why did you do that, Beth?"

She couldn't look at him. "I don't know."

"Bad move," he said.

"You don't want me here?"

"Forrest has more experience." That didn't exactly answer her question. But, then again, she had not really answered his. She couldn't. The answer was too complicated and too close to that part of her she protected.

"Well, I'm the best you got," she said.

"Fine, then let's get to work."

Beth had never seen Ty so focused. It had taken the evening and much of the night, but together they had tracked down and set up surveillance on eleven members of the Wolf Posse and their vehicles. From their efforts they had determined only three were in a position to be holding a captive.

When they pulled to a stop behind the only gas station in Koun'nde, it was officially Thursday morning, but so early even the roosters were still in bed. They parked here because there were other cars parked around and because it gave an excellent view of Oliver Boehm's residence. The posse member lived here alone. He was inside with Vernon Dent, and all the window coverings were closed. That could mean they were sleeping or just smoking weed. But it could also mean they had Abbie.

Beth consulted her list of the remaining gang members, furnished by Ty.

"Chino's too obvious," said Ty.

"So that leaves—" Beth consulted her pad of notes "—Oliver Boehm, Eric Goseyun and Geoffrey Corrales."

"Eric has been moving up in Faras's favor. He'd expect me to have Eric on my list. Oliver is reliable, but not the brightest of his men. Geoffrey, I don't know. He's young. Maybe twenty-one or so. But he's already impressed Faras with his ruthlessness. He's the one Faras sends to hurt people when Chino isn't available. His understudy." Ty swallowed. Of all the three remaining possibilities, Geoffrey Corrales was the man he most hoped Abbie was not with.

"We have to eliminate each one," said Beth. "That means getting into their places."

Her phone rang and she lifted it from her pocket.

"It's Forrest," she told him, and took the call. "Hoosay." She listened. "Good. Yes. All right. Let us know." She disconnected and turned her attention from Boehm's residence to him. "Your tribal council gave us permission to track the phones and conversations of all the names you provided."

"That's a lot of phones," he said.

"We might get something."

Ty shook his head. "I don't think so. Faras was too damn smart."

"Why do you think he is using you instead of Chino?" asked Beth.

"He needs Chino for protection."

"But he suspected Chino was out to take his place. Now he trusts him? And why you? Any one of his men would make a delivery, if asked."

"You've got a theory?"

She nodded. "I think he's going to let you make the delivery and then tip the police, throw you under the bus and make the whole mess go away."

"Handing me over to the police is stupid because I could turn on him."

"Not if you're dead."

Ty was silent as if letting that sink in. "Yeah, maybe."

"I have to admit, I was certain you were tied up in this."

"I *am* tied up in this."

"Yes, but not the way I expected. I believe I've convinced Forrest of your efforts to remain neutral, but there's a reason my boss isn't letting you make the delivery."

"He doesn't trust me."

"And he wants Usov. Your sister is secondary. He wouldn't have taken this operation if I had chosen the other. He's the boss and he goes where the action is."

"You get the leavings," said Ty.

"Exactly."

"But you didn't wait to have him assign you. You volunteered."

"Looks better. Don't you think?"

His expression showed he was unconvinced with her line of logic. Well, that was the best she could do.

Ty focused on Oliver Boehm's current residence, such as it was. The tilting double-wide had once belonged to Oliver's mother, who had died long ago, and it seemed very much as if neither she nor Oliver nor the tribe's HUD offices had done anything in the way of upkeep. The yellow grass grew high enough to cover the dirty, faded paint but not the torn screens or broken windows patched with cardboard.

"So, do you want me to try the front door to get a look inside one of those windows?"

Beth lifted her binoculars and stared toward Oliver's trailer. "I believe I can get inside through that back window."

"You mean the one covered with cardboard?" he asked.

She smiled. "Yeah, that's the one."

"I'll be outside the door. You holler if you find her or if you need me."

She handed him a radio. Then she clicked the side button. His radio relayed the sound. "You hear that and I need you to break in."

"Got it." He clipped the radio on his belt.

Next she offered him a pistol. He shook his head. He still carried no gun.

"I need you armed," she said.

He gave her a sad look. "I turned in my rifle when I got stateside, Beth, and I don't ever plan to aim a firearm at a human being again. Each one you kill takes part of your soul."

She motioned her head toward the trailer. "These men don't have souls."

"Everyone does."

They made their way to the trailer. Ty boosted Beth through the window and then moved to the door, standing off to the side.

The light was coming up and time was flying by. She returned her backup weapon to her coat pocket and left him.

Ty waited for what seemed like a week outside that door. The fact that he heard nothing was all that kept him waiting. His gaze was on the window, but he was alert to the sound of the front door click. The door cracked open and Beth stared back at him. She lifted a finger to her full lips and then stepped out.

"Oliver is there, passed out in the room I entered. The trailer is filthy, but empty."

"Cross him off the list."

Beth glanced up at the sky. "Jake should be making the drop soon."

They exchanged worried glances. Ty knew the danger of Jake's mission. He prayed that his brother came home safe and that Forrest succeeded in striking a blow at the Russian crime organization.

"Who next?" she asked. The clock was ticking. If any one of the Russians alerted Faras to trouble, Abbie's situation would only become more perilous.

"Eric Goseyun or Geoffrey Corrales?" she asked.

"I'd choose Corrales. He's more trustworthy and he's been with Faras longer."

But as it turned out they watched Geoffrey leave

his home and they followed him to the Wolf Posse headquarters. He could not be watching Abbie.

"Goseyun," said Ty, turning Jake's truck back toward Piñon Forks. In a few minutes they reached his place, on a circular dirt road with five other single-family homes, all built in the 1970s, of cinder block and painted beige. The yards were littered with broken plastic toys, grills and faded lawn chairs.

Ty slowed before making the circle. "No way to creep up on Goseyun."

"Also no way for his neighbors not to see him come or go."

"Front door?" asked Ty.

"Fastest way in." She drew out her badge.

"Don't use that. If we're wrong, word will get out."

She tucked the badge beneath her shirt as Ty parked in Goseyun's driveway behind a van. Had he taken Abbie in that vehicle? Ty's mouth went grim and his breathing increased.

Beth looked through the back window and then to him, shaking her head. Abbie was not inside the van.

She remained where she was, with a clear view of the main entrance, as Ty mounted the stairs and knocked.

Eric Goseyun appeared at the front door in a pair of sweatpants slung low on his narrow hips and a white tank top. He smiled at seeing Ty and looked completely at ease. His eyes were dull and bloodshot. There was a definite odor of weed clinging to him. His long hair hung limp and the yellowish color of his skin seemed to be the harbinger of illness.

"Yo, bro. What's happening?"

"Delivering a message from Faras." Ty did not wait to be asked in but stepped past Eric into his house. Before entering he waved Beth away. It was her turn to wait outside and wonder.

"Why don't he just call me, bro?" Goseyun offered his joint, thus far held behind his back.

Ty waved away the offer. "You know that Fed, Forrest? The one supposed to be looking in to the dam collapse?"

"Yeah, I heard about him," said Goseyun.

"He's looking at Faras for the missing girls."

"Wow. That's bad."

"So don't call him. You got something to say, say it in person."

"Yeah, sure thing."

Ty thumbed toward the bedrooms. "Mind if I use the can?"

"No, go on. Sorry about the smell. Got a broken pipe or something."

Ty headed off and turned to see Goseyun reach his sagging couch and drop into the cushions, completely at ease. Then Ty searched the place.

As he had suspected, Goseyun's place was filthy, but Abbie was not here. Ty went back outside and, with Beth, returned to his vehicle, slipping into the driver's seat.

"That's all of them," he said, in confusion. The Wolf Posse had more members than tribal police and he had checked each one. Time was ticking away. As soon as the Russians failed to contact Faras about a successful drop, Faras would know Ty had failed. Then he would hurt Abbie. His heart now ached in his chest and his throat was tight.

Ty grabbed his hair at each side of his temple, feeling the sticky gel as he clenched his fists.

"What about the women?" Beth asked.

He straightened as the fog of panic lifted from his brain. He turned to face her. Her expression was open, thoughtful. No panic, all business.

"What?" he asked.

"Women," she repeated. "Female members of the gang."

Ty gripped the wheel and gave it a shake, bringing himself forward and then back against the seat.

"Yes! I know where she is," she said.

Ty met her gaze with one of wonder. She was so smart. He'd been lost, sinking as he faced failure, and she'd just turned them in a new direction. The right direction. He knew it and now his heart pounded in anticipation.

Ty set them in motion toward the alpha female of the Wolf Posse, certain that his sister was in the care of Jewell Tasa.

Chapter Twenty

Jewell had a private place between Koun'nde and Turquoise Ridge. She liked horses and Faras made sure she had several. But he couldn't buy her what she most coveted. Jewell wanted the title of Miss Indian Rodeo Queen. She could qualify, being from a federally recognized tribe and being over the age of eighteen. She'd have no trouble raising the money to compete because Faras would hand it to her. But that did not mean she would win. She'd have to enroll in college and she'd have to impress the judges with her horsemanship, among other things.

Ty pulled the silver pickup off the road and pointed to the ranch house with a small horse barn and new fencing corralling four fine horses. A large satellite dish on the western side of the house ensured that Jewell had internet, phone and cable.

"That livestock belong to Jewell?" asked Beth.

"Her pride and joy," he answered.

"Looks like great collateral."

He liked the way she thought. "You'd have to catch

them first. The chestnut is her favorite. She calls him Big Red."

"I've been around horses most of my life. I can get that horse haltered and ready."

They discussed strategy as precious seconds leaked away. The dashboard clock told him that Jake and Forrest should be making contact with the Russians. It was going down right now.

"We better be right," said Ty.

Beth gazed at the house with her binoculars. "She's got a look-out."

"Where?"

She offered the glasses and pointed. He spotted Randy, her kid brother, throwing a ball against the side of the barn. Ty glanced at the clock on the dash. It was almost nine in the morning. He should be in school. Beth was right. He already knew that Randy was a solid worker and just the right age to be inconspicuous.

"I'll get him clear before I go in," said Ty. He had no interest in hurting children, but he knew how effective they were as members of the gang.

Ty stared at the house. He no longer just wanted to rescue Abbie. He wanted the Wolf Posse eliminated. He wanted to take out those who sold their children and kidnapped his sister. Ty was done walking the line because that was not what lines were for. They were for crossing.

"Ready?" he asked.

Beth checked her pistol and then nodded. Then she crouched down out of sight as Ty drove them the short distance to the house, parking out of view on the side of the barn. Before they were completely stopped, Beth was out of the truck and running along the side of the building. She disappeared before Randy's reflection appeared in his side mirror.

"Jake?" Randy called. "That you?"

Ty's phone rang. It was Jake. He took the call as Randy approached from the back of the truck.

"Yeah," Ty said.

It was Jake's voice. Just hearing him caused Ty to squeeze his eyes shut and blow out a breath of sweet relief.

"We're done. Got four members of the crime organization, all alive, and they didn't have time to destroy their computers or cell phones. We got it all, Ty."

Ty couldn't speak past the lump.

"Do you have her? Did you find Abbie?"

"Jake?" Randy spoke from beside Ty's open window.

"Not yet. I'll call soon." He ended the call and turned to Randy, whose eyes were now widening.

"Ty!" he said, and backed away from the door.

Ty slipped out to stand before him in the tall grass. Randy looked back toward the house. He'd misjudged the situation and the distance, finding himself out of sight of the house and facing Ty instead of a tribal police officer.

"Your sister home?" he asked.

From somewhere in the pasture, he heard the sound of a tin can being shaken with what sounded like oats. Ty was certain that Beth would soon have her pick of the horses.

Randy redirected his attention to Ty.

"She's got her period. Ma sent me over to take care of her."

"That right?" Ty closed the distance.

"She don't want to see no one," said Randy, backing up as he spoke.

"Not smart to come up to the truck, Randy. It's a Trojan horse."

"A what?"

"See, if you were in school, you'd learn about stuff like this. Didn't I tell you to stay in school?"

"Yeah." He glanced toward the house, no longer in sight. "Listen, I gotta go. My sister…"

With his head turned, he never saw Ty strike. Before Randy could call out, Ty had him against his chest with one hand over his mouth. The boy's struggles were ineffective.

"I'm not going to hurt you, Randy. But you aren't warning Jewell."

In short order, he had Randy tied hand and foot and secured to a sturdy fence post. His mouth was gagged with the cloth Ty had worn in his hair.

"Quit wiggling. It only tightens the knots, and that post will give you slivers."

Ty left Randy and headed for the house. The front door was unlocked, owing to the fact that Jewell did not expect company and was confident that Randy would alert her if there was any.

He found her lying on the couch watching afternoon soaps.

"Ty! What a nice surprise." She glanced behind him toward the door. "You see my brother outside?"

"He's tied up."

Jewell rose from the couch, assessing him now with her large intelligent eyes.

"Where is she?" Ty asked.

"I don't know what you're talking about." Her eyes shifted, telling him otherwise.

"My sister. Get her," said Ty.

Jewell's laugh was forced. "She's not here."

"That so?"

Jewell lifted her chin in a gesture that some women used as a display of arrogance and disdain. "Get out of here."

"My sister?"

She waved an impatient hand and Ty saw her nail polish was black. "Search the place if you want."

"I don't have time for that."

"Faras finds out you've been bothering me and he'll take you out. I don't know why he lets you hang with us anyway. You're not one of us and your brother's a cop."

Ty was done talking. He grabbed Jewell by the upper arm and forced her to the door.

"Hey! Let go of me." She struggled but still hurried along beside him. "Faras's gonna kill you for this."

He took her through the open door and to the yard, where she had a clear view of her barn and pasture.

"Where's my brother?" she asked, her voice losing the fury and taking on notes of panic.

Ty did not answer.

"Beth!" he called.

FBI Agent Hoosay stepped from the barn wearing her body armor, looking tough and oh, so sexy to Ty. He tucked that image away for another time, hoping they both lived long enough for him to enjoy it.

Beth had her pistol drawn. In her opposite hand, she held the red nylon rope of a lead. She made a clicking sound and came out leading Big Red.

Jewell gasped and lifted her free hand to her heart. Beth raised her pistol and pressed it at the horse's head just below the ear.

"All right." Jewell threw up her hands. "She's here. I'll get her. Where's my brother?"

"Abbie first," said Ty.

Jewell turned toward the house and he walked with her. A glance showed Beth's pistol holstered. She held the horse, by a loose lead, and gently stroked his cheek.

Ty allowed Jewell to take him upstairs. She moved the large wooden linen cabinet, which was on rollers. He released her so she could move the rack of towels and makeup to reveal a small door cut in the wall. It was closed with a bolt.

Jewell motioned with her head. "She's in there."

"Get her." Ty held his breath as he worried what he would find. If she'd hurt Abbie, he didn't know if he could control himself.

Jewell threw back the bolt and tugged open the

door. There was no sound from within the dark crawl space. She reached and tugged a beaded pull chain, snapping on the single lightbulb.

Ty crouched and saw a large dog crate on the dusty floor. Inside, Abbie lay on her side on a blanket, facing away from them, unmoving.

"What's wrong with her?" asked Ty.

"I give her some cough medicine, the kind with codeine and alcohol. It keeps her quiet."

"Get her," he ordered, pushing Jewell toward the cubby.

She crawled to his sister, opened the crate and rolled Abbie to her back. Ty gasped at the gray pallor of her face.

Was she breathing?

"Wakey, wakey, Abbie. You've got company."

Abbie's eyes blinked open and Ty let his head drop back. He could breathe again.

He heard a light tread on the stairs. A glance to the hall showed Beth on the stairs, gun drawn.

"It's me," said Beth, coming to the landing and heading for him. "You okay?"

He nodded and turned his attention back to the bathroom.

Jewell was yanking a very groggy Abbie from her prison. Ty stooped and gathered Abbie to him. She smelled of sweat and tears and alcohol. Ty kicked the small door shut.

"Hey!" shouted Jewell.

Beth threw the bolt shut. "She have her phone?"

"No. It's downstairs on the coffee table."

Ty raised his voice. "Jewell, when you see Faras, remember that I have Randy."

The pounding ceased.

"I have to bring her in as well," said Beth.

Ty spoke to Jewell, cautioning her. Then he let her out. Beth took it from there and in short order Jewell's hands were cuffed behind her back. Ty preceded her down the stairs, carrying his little sister in his arms. She stopped in the living room to take Jewell's phone.

Once outside, Ty set Abbie carefully in the truck cab as Beth ordered Jewell to lie down on the ground. Then Beth saw to Randy. She took off his gag, replaced the ropes with zip ties on his wrists and delivered him to the truck cab.

Ty was in the cab trying to get Abbie to stay awake when Beth ordered the boy into the cab. Randy hesitated.

"Is that Abbie?" asked Randy, the shock evident in his voice. Ty realized that Randy and Abbie were likely in the same grade at school.

"Didn't you know?" asked Ty.

Randy shook his head and began to cry.

"Get in, Randy. Hold Abbie up," said Ty.

Beth spoke from the open passenger door. "I'm putting Jewell in the back."

"She might jump."

"I'll cuff her to your brother's tool kit."

Jake's tool kit was stainless steel, bolted down and went from one side of the bed to the other. Jewell would not be able to escape it.

Ty exited the vehicle to help Beth secure Jewell.

Then they returned to the truck cab. Abbie sprawled across Randy's lap.

He gave Ty an apologetic look. "I can't hold her on account of the cuffs."

Beth climbed in and pulled Abbie across her lap, then secured the seat belt around Randy. Then Ty set them in motion.

"We have to get them to tribal before Faras finds out that his whole world just went sideways."

Ty set them in motion. Randy sat sullen beside Ty sniffing occasionally and Abbie slumped against Beth.

"Call Kee," said Ty. "Tell him I have Abbie and that she's on something."

Beth lifted her phone at the same time Jewell's mobile played a popular rap song about the boss.

"Faras," she said, looking at the screen.

They didn't answer and the call cut out, followed by a text that displayed on the lock screen.

No word from R. Bring her.

"R? Is that Russians?" asked Beth.

"Possibly."

"He knows. And we got him," said Beth, lifting Jewell's phone. She called Kee first. Ty listened as she gave him the important details. She disconnected and turned to him. "He'll meet us at your tribal health clinic." She made a call to her field office, reporting the successful recovery of Abigail Redhorse and listening while Ty wondered what she knew. He didn't have long to wait, but the call seemed endless. They flew through Koun'nde under stormy gray skies and were heading for Piñon Forks when she disconnected.

"Jake is safe. They have the Russians in custody, including Victor Vitoli. He's the one Mills called when they had issues. Forrest was hoping to bag him because Vitoli answers directly to Usov." Beth blew through pursed lips, a sound of relief.

"Where are they?" asked Ty.

"Still in Darabee, but Forrest is sending all available agents to the Wolf Posse's headquarters to make arrests."

"The missing? Garcia, Espinoza and Kesselman?" asked Ty.

"Not there."

Ty knew that Marta Garcia was a close friend of Kacey. She had risked her life to get Marta free.

"Maybe we'll get something from the Russians' tech. We have very good people. They could still find them," said Beth.

Ty wanted more. He wanted that organization shut down for good and all the girls that they had taken to be returned to their families.

They reached the clinic to find Kee waiting on the sidewalk, pacing beside Lori. Kee had Beth's door open the instant Ty put the truck in Park.

"Jake back yet?" he asked Lori.

Lori cast him a worried gaze. "All en route to the posse according to Ava."

As the tribe's new dispatcher, Ava knew where all the officers were at all times.

Beth passed Abbie to Kee. He took her to the waiting stretcher, removing his coat to place it around his little sister. Then he began checking her vitals as Lori pushed them toward the side entrance on the women's health care side of the clinic.

Beth left Randy, who sat with head bowed as tears splashed the denim of his jeans, leaving dark spots. Ty paused beside Beth to speak to Randy.

"Ask for Bear Den," said Ty. "He'll help you, Randy, if you let him. You hear me?"

Randy sniffed and nodded.

With all the tribal police on their way to Wolf Posse headquarters, Beth had to bring Jewell to the tribal police herself. Ty hesitated as Beth took the driver's seat, torn between following Kee and following her.

"Call your mother. Tell her we have your sister," said Beth. "I'll be right back."

"Okay," answered Ty, and he followed Kee and his sister.

Beth drove Jewell and Randy from the clinic lot to the one before headquarters. Randy waited beside the truck as she released his sister from the toolbox, then neatly snapped the cuffs back together behind her back. She assisted Jewell down and found Ava Hood taking charge of Randy. Beth walked Jewell into the station, stopping at the dispatch desk while Ava retrieved the keys to the only cell on the premises.

Ava lifted the headset to report Beth's arrival to Tinnin. Beth deposited Randy in the squad room beside Ava's desk. Beth knew the woman had been a detective in Salt River and would know how to process a prisoner, even a minor one.

Beth escorted Jewell down the hall and happily deposited her in the cell, loving that satisfying click of the lock engaging. Then she returned to dispatch.

"I called protective services," said Ava. "They're sending someone for Randy."

Beth nodded and then kneeled before Randy. "You aren't your sister, kiddo. You can make choices. The gang is gone. You're not."

Ava used a tissue to wipe Randy's running nose.

Beth was already on her way out and Ty had to jog over to catch her.

"You going to the clinic?" she asked.

"I did. Abbie is doing all right. Kee's got her, so I'm going with you," he said.

"Your mom?"

"On her way. I want to see Faras arrested."

Beth cast Ty a winning smile. "Just what I was thinking."

Unfortunately, they arrived too late to be of much use, but just in time to see Faras led to Jake's police cruiser in handcuffs. Ty met his gaze as Faras did a double take at Ty's clothing and appearance. Ty felt satisfaction at seeing his former friend in handcuffs and he found gratification in knowing that Faras would no longer be preying on their people.

It took the rest of the day for the FBI and tribal police to round up all the Wolf Posse members.

Beth was back in her element as she and Forrest

began the process of interrogating the suspects, starting with the Russians.

Ty felt like a fifth wheel. Beth no longer needed him. The creeping realization dawned that she would never need him. He had served his purpose, helped her make the kind of case that would bring her notice, accolades and the transfer to a major field office that she so coveted. In helping her reach her dreams, he would lose her forever. It was in that moment of crystallizing awareness that he admitted to himself that he loved Beth and that, as usual, his life choices stank. Just once he'd like to make a move that didn't end up kicking him back in the...teeth.

Ty left Jake's truck at tribal headquarters and walked to the clinic alone. Not that anyone noticed he was missing. Once inside, he found Kee. It was now after hours and Abbie was the only patient still here.

"How's she doing?" he asked.

"She's good. Whatever they gave her is wearing off. She's tired, bruised and hungry."

"Hungry is good," said Ty, the gratitude at his sister's recovery warming him.

Ty looked around. "Where's Mom?"

"Did you call her?" asked Kee.

"I did. But that was a while ago." Confusion morphed into a cold panic. It was hours ago.

Kee's voice held a note of concern. "I was going to call, but it got crazy busy here and..."

Ty phoned the house and got no answer. He disconnected and met Kee's worried gaze.

"Call Jake. Send him to Mom," said Ty, running back toward the door.

"What? Why?" called Kee.

He paused to look back at his brother's worried face. "Dad. His parole."

"Oh, no!" said Kee.

Chapter Twenty-One

Ty reached his childhood home in Jake's pickup and immediately spotted a problem with Burt's truck. The driver's side door gaped and Ty's worry solidified into certainty. His father was here. Ty narrowed his eyes, finding no unfamiliar vehicle. The absence did not reassure him. His father didn't have a truck of his own. In fact, he would have only what possessions had been returned to him upon release. Likely he got here by bus or caught a ride.

Ty thought back to that day when he was convicted, picturing the sports jacket, shirt and jeans. His father's appearances in court had been the only time he'd ever seen his father dressed like that.

He took his foot off the gas and the truck glided past his mother's place. His dad did not know Jake's truck, and if Ty didn't stop, he might not realize he had company. He glanced at the dashboard clock, which read 6:00 p.m. The Doka girls, fostering with his mom, should all be home from school. As if having their mother arrested for drug trafficking was not enough, now his father had broken into their life.

Ty fumed as he acknowledged that in one way he and his father were alike. They were both dangerous when angry. But unlike his father, Ty preferred to settle scores without the other party knowing Ty had done anything at all. He'd pulled that off once with his father. He'd never do it again. But he didn't need to broadcast his arrival.

Ty parked behind the neighbors' place and crept through the backyard, past the fire pit and the circle of mismatched lawn chairs. He reached the rear door and paused, squatting below the level of the windows. The daylight had faded, and in the twilight it would be difficult for anyone inside to see out. But if the lights were on, it would be perfect for him to see in.

He lifted himself up high enough to peer inside. He knew his mother did not lock the doors except at night, so it was likely still open. Nothing moved inside the kitchen. At this hour, his mother should be preparing supper, but the room was empty. Her absence here was as worrisome as her absence from Abbie's bedside.

The knob was cold in his hand as he slowly turned it. A moment later he was inside.

"Leave him be, Colton!" That was his mother's voice and Colton was what she had always called Ty's father. The idea of fighting his father turned his stomach as much as the belief that he might very well lose. Like him, Colton Redhorse did not fight fair.

Ty continued through the empty kitchen toward the sound of his mother's voice. He'd forgotten the way her voice went high and quavered when she confronted her ex-husband's rages.

"I got your message. Divorce papers, order of protection. Funny, but no one asked me if I wanted a divorce."

Where was Burt? Ty wondered as he tried to push back the terrible possibilities that rose in his mind. His father would not tolerate a rival.

"This sack of turd is my replacement?" asked his father. There was the thumping sound of something striking something hollow, followed by a groan.

Burt, Ty suspected, was down.

There was a cry from one of the Doka girls, followed by his father's shout.

"Shut up!"

How often had his father told him the same thing?

Ty stepped into plain view, his gaze sweeping the living room. His mother sat on the very edge of her chair beside her cane, her damaged foot wrapped in its special stocking with gauze covering the place where her amputated toes should have been. His mother's diabetes made her dizzy and weak at times and the surgeries decreased her mobility.

On the floor between the coffee table and his mother's chair was Burt Rope. Burt was motionless, bleeding from a head wound, and seemed to be only semiconscious.

The three Doka girls, Jackie, Shirley and Winnie, were all huddled together on the floor before the muted television. Behind them, the evening news flashed video of other tragedies. Ty focused on the one unfolding before him.

His father had not seen him yet, as his back was to Ty and he was concentrating on winding up to kick Burt again.

"Welcome home, Pop," said Ty, leaning indolently on the door frame.

Colton Redhorse spun about.

"Kee?" he asked.

Ty smirked. "Nope."

"Ty. Should have known from that grin. I'll get to you in a minute." He turned back to Burt.

"No. You'll get to me now."

Colton turned, his expression filled with anticipation. His dark eyes glittered and a smile lifted his mouth. He was looking forward to this. Ty managed not to take a step backward as he met his father's cold stare, but it was hard.

"Figured it out. Took a while because you're so slick. But I finally worked it through." Colton turned to May, who had slipped off the chair and kneeled beside Burt. "Get away from him."

His father pulled a gun from his waistband and pointed it at Burt. May complied, dragging herself up and back to her chair. When Ty's father turned back, Ty was three steps closer.

Ty lifted a finger at the pistol and then pointed to Burt. "Got three parole violations that I see. B and E, weapon and assault. Not your best start."

"Shut up," said Colton, and turned the gun on Ty as he spoke to May. "You know what your son did? He set me up. Crashed on purpose so we'd all get caught. What they call that? Cut off his nose despite his face."

"To spite his face," Ty said, correcting him.

"Shut up," said Colton. That was his favorite expression, his easy go-to.

Ty spoke to the Doka children. "Girls, I want you to walk behind me and out the back door."

They rose, but Colton turned his pistol in their direction.

"Abbie stays," he said.

He'd last seen Abbie when she was eight years old. It was no surprise that he could not recognize her.

"Like I've been telling you," said his mother.

"Shut up," barked Colton.

"Those are foster kids. None of them is Abbie," said Ty.

His father glared at him. "Why should I believe anything you say?"

Ty motioned to the girls to come to him with one hand. Jackie pushed her younger siblings ahead of her. They rushed past Ty and out the back door a moment later.

"Fine, go on," said Colton, closing the door after the cow was out of the barn.

Ty had hoped that he wouldn't shoot children, but his father's temper had not improved with his incarceration and he had never looked more fit. Ty, on the other hand, was still recovering from the lacerations on his shoulder.

"Where's Abbie?" Colton raged. "I want to see my little girl."

"Faras Pike kidnapped her to get my cooperation."

May cried out and then began to weep.

"Faras? That little turd. He's next on my list."

His father would have to stand in line behind the FBI, thought Ty.

"You want to call him?" Ty offered his phone.

Colton grinned. "My message needs to be delivered in person."

Ty slipped his phone into his back pocket.

"How about you and I settle this outside?" asked Ty.

"You're my son, but you betrayed me. Betrayed your own father. So I'm going to return the favor, make 'em open those closed records." He turned the grip of the pistol toward Burt. Then he wiped the trigger and grip with his shirttails. Ty had an inkling of what Colton planned as his father crouched beside Burt's still form and pressed the pistol into his limp fingers.

"That won't fool anyone," said Ty.

"Shut up."

Ty had been told that just one too many times. He kicked his father's arm, sending the gun thumping across the carpet, but Colton grabbed Ty's leg and twisted, sending Ty sprawling to the floor.

His father roared and dove onto Ty. During the wrestling match, Ty only once had his father in a headlock, but was quickly tossed by the man who outweighed him by fifty pounds of muscle.

His mother struggled to get Burt to his feet. Ty wished she'd leave Burt and run, but she didn't. When

Colton reached for her, Ty landed a body blow to his exposed ribs. His father expelled the air from his lungs and caved toward the blow. His mother was up and Burt gained his feet as the two shuffled out the front door. Ty blocked his father's pursuit with his body and his father changed direction, retrieving the pistol.

Colton aimed the weapon at Ty and ordered him to move. Ty didn't. Colton roared as he holstered the weapon in the front of his jeans. Then he charged Ty, the tackle sending them both out the door, Ty flying backward. Ty caught a glimpse of his mother on the hard ground first beside Burt, who was on his hands and knees, retching.

His father twisted and grabbed something at his hip. Ty saw the flash of steel. His father had a knife. He needed to keep his father from hurting his mother. Sending him to prison had worked but only for a while. He was back, he was a wild animal and he needed to be put down. But Ty did not know if he could do it. A primal part of him resisted until Colton's gaze locked on his mother. Then something broke inside him.

Ty lunged for the blade, capturing his father's wrist in both hands. His father released the weapon. They rolled over and over, out into the yard. Colton came up on top, straddling him and tugging the pistol from the front of his jeans.

Colton's eyes blazed with triumph. "Still the better man," he growled, and then lifted the pistol, pressing the barrel to the center of Ty's forehead.

Ty kept his eyes wide open. The gunshot made him jump.

There was another shot, followed by another.

He shouldn't have heard that, not if the bullet passed through his skull. He stared up at his father, at first thinking his dad had shot wide just to scare him.

Colton's arms hung at his sides and he gaped at Ty with a look of confusion etched on his brow. Ty's attention moved to the red stains blooming by the second on the front of his father's blue denim shirt. Colton tipped sideways and fell beside Ty. Behind his father stood FBI Special Agent Beth Hoosay, her gold badge swinging before her and her arms outstretched, holding her pistol.

BETH STARED IN shock at Colton Redhorse's inert form. She'd discharged three rounds, fearing all the while that she might hit Ty. The cold panic still froze her from the inside out and she stood motionless, pistol still aimed at Colton Redhorse's body.

Neither man had heard her approach or her order for Colton to drop his weapon. Only May Redhorse had looked in her direction, seen her run across the lawn and draw her sidearm, shouting that she was FBI.

Kee had phoned her, told her what had happened. During that drive, racing from Darabee to his mother's home, all she could think of was that she'd be too late. Too late to save Ty. Too late to reach the conclusion that she didn't want a promotion if it meant losing him. Too late to understand what was really important in her life…who was really important. And too late to have a chance to tell him that she loved him with all her ambitious imperfect self.

Beth stood staring at Colton Redhorse, waiting for him to move or groan or try to hurt Ty again. Her finger began to cramp upon the trigger. If he moved, she'd shoot him again right in the back.

Colton Redhorse didn't move because her training was too good and her reflexes too programmed not to hit center mass. Now there would be an inquiry into this shooting, as there was with all cases when an agent used deadly force. But instead of considering the implications to her career, she could think only of how close she had come to losing Ty forever.

Would he forgive her for killing his father or would he thank her? Ty understood about protecting his family, and they were a wonderful family. Getting to know them all made her long for what she had missed being an only child. Every one of his family had treated her with the respect and acceptance she thought could only be found in her career. What was a career set against the potential of the man before her?

Ty had shown her his capacity to love. He loved his mother and his sister. He'd protected everyone in his family at great personal expense. He was a shining example of brains and heart. And she knew she'd never find another man like him.

Ty shoved his father the rest of the way off him. There was the sound of sirens heading toward them. His brother Jake was coming. The whole tribal police was coming, but they'd all been out between Turquoise Ridge and Koun'nde. Darabee had been closer and she'd driven like a madwoman. Her backup pulled in, Agent Forrest exiting his vehicle with his service weapon drawn.

Ty checked his father's pulse and then left him to move to his mother and Mr. Rope. Ty never looked at Beth or even acknowledged her presence. His shoulder was bleeding again, but he didn't seem to notice that, either, as he gathered his weeping mother in his arms.

Beth kept her weapon on Colton Redhorse as Forrest placed a foot on the perp's weapon and then stooped to retrieve it. He also checked the man's pulse and shook his head, eyes on her.

"Clear," he said.

She holstered her pistol and expelled a long breath. The next one came fast and rasping. The adrenaline, previously contained to the narrow focus of her suspect, now released into her nervous system, giving her a trembling, disjointed feeling that surged through her with increasing ferocity.

"Is he...?" Her voice had lifted an octave. Nothing in her training had prepared her for the moment she took a life.

Forrest nodded.

The yard filled up with law enforcement vehicles, headlights shone across the yellow grass, casting long shadows before her. Ty and May's faces turned blue and red as the lights from the police vehicles flashed. Officer Redhorse jogged past her to his mother while Ty saw to Burt Rope, getting him to his seat to await the incoming ambulance. Beth just stood there watching the chaos as her ears buzzed.

Forrest approached, touching her elbow. "You all right?"

"Never shot anyone before," she said.

It didn't feel good, and even knowing it was necessary and that Colton Redhorse was a dangerous man, she felt ill. Suddenly Beth understood Ty's insistence to never hold a firearm.

"Feel sick."

"Yeah. I know," said Forrest.

He ushered her to his vehicle and opened the passenger side door, pressing her into the seat. "Going to need you to make a statement. Man, you got here fast. Never seen anyone drive like that. I lost you on the switchbacks between here and Darabee."

Switchbacks? She didn't even remember them. She lifted a trembling hand, extending her fingers to show him.

"That normal?" she asked.

"It hits everyone differently. But always after the danger is past. You did your job, Agent Hoosay."

That was a nice way of saying it. But she hadn't been doing her job. Her flight here and the shooting had been personal. Only her training had ensured that she announced herself and followed the rules of engagement. But she would have shot Colton Redhorse regardless and the fact that she shot him in the back mattered to her not at all.

"Listen, I'm going to have the EMTs have a look at you."

"Is Ty all right?" She tried to see past Forrest, who squatted before her. There were so many people here now and Ty was lost in the crowd.

"He's with his brother Jake. I have to set up the perimeter."

Perimeter? Yes, that was what needed to be done.

"His mom and the girls?"

"The girls are all scared but safe. Burt will need a trip to the ER. But I'm sure he'll recover."

"Can I see Ty?"

"Not now. We need his statement first. You wait here a while, okay?"

No. Not okay. She put her head in her hands and took some deep breaths. She just needed a minute.

Chapter Twenty-Two

What a car wreck, thought Ty. Two hours after the shooting, he waited in the interrogation room, the only one in the small tribal police headquarters. The walls were white and the floor a scuffed gray tile. Furniture consisted of two chairs, one with a student-style, flip-up desk. He sat in the other, the one where the occupant was not required to take notes. A glance at the mirror showed only his reflection. His hair was disheveled, his cheek bruised and his T-shirt bloody from the wound that just would not stay closed. Kee would be mad at him about that again, no doubt.

Ty had been here before, once too often. This time he was not handcuffed...yet.

He'd wanted to help Beth make her case, her career and gain her ticket out of the field office where she had reached as far as she could. FBI agents advanced by making a big case. But he sure had never intended to have his dysfunctional family as the center of her investigation.

His father was dead and his overwhelming emotion was relief. The man who had terrorized his family and beaten his mother would never hurt them again. But the scars he left behind would take time to heal. His mother and Burt had gone by ambulance to the tribe's clinic, where Kee would be seeing to their injuries. Abbie was already there. Kee's family had become some of his best customers, and that was no coveted position.

He wondered if Shirley, Jackie and Winnie were all right and he wondered how many nightmares would follow from this evening's events. Had they seen Ty's father shot down like the rabid animal that he was?

The door opened and Ty shifted, lifting his chin in a weary acceptance that things would get worse before they got better. Three men stepped into the small room, Kenshaw Little Falcon, their medicine man and a certified therapist, Police Chief Wallace Tinnin, chewing gum and rocking awkwardly on his booted foot, and FBI Agent Luke Forrest. Ty looked toward the hall but Beth did not appear, and Forrest closed the door.

They wanted his statement. He wanted some answers. They indulged him. He learned that Abbie was dehydrated but otherwise healthy…physically, that is. Jewell Tasa had been charged with kidnapping and currently occupied the tribe's only jail cell right down the hall. Ty's mother was being treated for a spike in her blood pressure and Burt was recovering from a head wound and broken ribs. The Doka girls had been seen by Kee and released to Hazel Tran, one of their tribal council members and the retired teacher who had been fostering their younger brothers, Hewett and

Jeffery. The Doka family was together again, except for their big sister Kacey, still in witness protection with Ty's brother Colt.

Forrest answered all of Ty's questions. Except the one he didn't ask—where was Beth?

Tinnin took over. "We got Faras and all members of the Wolf Posse under arrest. They've been transported to the Darabee jail under Detective Bear Den's supervision."

Ty had no doubt that the posse would not be seen by visitors of any sort while Bear Den was in charge. "Randy Tasa?"

"Protective services picked him up. He'll be placed with a family on the rez in a day or two," said Kenshaw.

"So," said Tinnin. "We need to take your statement."

"Starting where?" asked Ty.

"Go through your day, searching for your sister with Agent Hoosay."

"Where is she?" he asked.

"Debriefing. Statements," said Forrest. "Same as you."

"Can I see her?"

Forrest shook his head.

Ty sighed and then gave them what they came for, going through the events of the day and their search for his sister, ending with their successful recovery of Abbie from a dog crate. He wondered if he'd ever be able to think about that without the scalding fury filling his stomach like boiling sap.

They released him a little before 10:00 p.m. with instructions to return in the morning for a second round of questioning. Jake took him over to the clinic for treatment. Kee scolded him as he opted for Steri-Strips instead of stitches or staples.

"If you're just going to keep tearing them out, this will work best. That cut will leave a scar. Don't blame me. It's your fault."

"Most things are," he muttered, the weariness settling between his shoulders.

Kee looked at him with wide eyes. Ty cocked his head in confusion and then watched in surprise as Kee's dark eyes filled with tears. Despite his injury, Kee hugged him, holding him tight as the sobs came.

Ty looked to Jake, who stood with his hands on his utility belt, his own eyes swimming.

"You saved Abbie," Jake said. "You found her and brought her home safe and you saved Mom."

Jake stepped forward to join the hug. Ty lifted his free hand to pat his older and younger brothers in turn.

Kee drew back first and yanked a tissue from the stainless-steel cart beside the examining table.

Jake pulled back and dropped his gaze to the floor as he spoke. "We just found out what you did."

The myriad of possibilities filled Ty's mind, but he kept mute, unsure as to what Jake referred to.

"Dad," clarified Jake, meeting his gaze. "Driving Dad and hitting that pole. You did it on purpose to get him out of our life."

Ty's eyes rounded, but he inclined his chin.

"And you helped me protect my baby girl," said Jake, "when the posse came after my baby."

"I couldn't have gotten Ava out of the hands of those Russian mobsters without you," added Kee.

"And he made sure Colt was in place to save Kacey," Jake said to Kee. Then he turned to Ty. "I'm sorry I didn't understand. That all this time I thought you were one of them."

"He's always been one of us," said Kee. "Always."

Ty's throat tightened. They were seeing him as if for the first time, recognizing his value, and their gratitude tore him up inside. He didn't know what to say.

"Does Mom know?" asked Ty at last.

"She said she knew all along. Suspected, at least, that you were the reason our dad was locked up," said Jake. "I don't know why she didn't tell me."

"Is she here?" Ty asked.

"Spending the night in the clinic with Abbie," said Kee. "Burt, too."

"Her house is still an active crime scene," added Jake. He rested a hand on Ty's uninjured shoulder. "They're gone now, the posse. Finished."

Ty let that soak in. All his life they had been there, this dark black hole that swallowed up their youth and from which they could not escape. But he and the tribe had done what couldn't be managed before. The Wolf Posse was no more.

"We have to make sure they aren't replaced by another gang," said Ty.

Jake smiled. "Might be a good job for you."

Ty shook his head, not understanding what he could do.

"All this time," said Jake, "I was looking up to Wallace Tinnin and Jack Bear Den, when you were right there in front of me. I feel so stupid."

"He was behind you," said Kee. "Behind all of us. That's why we couldn't see him."

Ty placed a hand over his mouth to keep them from seeing his trembling lower lip.

"Can I see Abbie and Ma?" he asked.

Ty was back at tribal headquarters the next morning and greeted by Kee's girl, Ava Hood.

"They're waiting for you in the chief's office," she said.

A step up from the interrogation room, he thought.

"Good work, Ty," said Ava, and gave him a warm smile.

This feeling of pride was so new to him he didn't know what to do with it.

"Thanks," he said, and ducked his head, making his way across the squad room.

On the way he was congratulated by Officer Harold Shay and thanked by Officer Daniel Wetselline. Detective Jack Bear Den stood at the chief's office and extended his hand. Ty took it and accepted both the handshake and Bear Den's sincere thanks to him for coming in.

Ty felt as if he'd stepped into some alternate universe, where he was no longer a "known associate of the Wolf Posse" and a potential threat to the tribe. It felt so odd and he was uncomfortable in his own skin.

One glance told him that Beth Hoosay was still not here. It seemed they were intentionally keeping them apart. Or perhaps Beth knew better than to buy the hometown-hero bit. Perhaps she did not wish to see him again, not even to say goodbye.

Tinnin waited for Ty to be seated in front of the large wooden desk that seemed to have survived from another century.

"It's possible that Chino Aria might testify in exchange for a deal. He would be tried here in our court system. What's your opinion on that?" Tinnin asked.

Ty tried to think of the last time anyone had asked his opinion on anything other than auto paint color and came up short. "He's dangerous. Wanted to take over the posse. If he's out, he'll try to build it again."

Bear Den met the chief's gaze and there was a silent exchange. Ty surmised that this was the opinion of at least one of them.

"What about the others?" asked Ty.

"The rest will be turned over to the DA for federal prosecution."

It was a break from past practices. The tribal leadership tried very diligently to take care of all violations of law. But they had never faced an organization that preyed on their women and worked with a notorious criminal organization.

"That's a good move," said Ty.

They reviewed his statement with him and he signed it.

"Anything else?" asked Tinnin.

"Randy Tasa?" asked Ty.

"Yeah, he's in some trouble. But we'll handle it within the tribe."

Ty approved of that. Even considered taking Randy under his wing. The boy reminded Ty of himself at times, trying to please and fit in and look out for his sister even when she was a mess and far beyond his help.

The last question was hardest. "Will I be seeing Beth Hoosay again?"

"Not officially," said Forrest. "She's been retrieved by the Oklahoma field office. She'll complete her work on this case from there."

Ty thought he did not succeed in keeping the emotions from showing in his expression. What did you do with a broken heart when it fell into your lap before a roomful of tough, seasoned lawmen?

"Doesn't stop you from seeing her unofficially," said Tinnin.

Ty met his gaze and then let it slip away. He was not going to chase after Beth unless she made it known that the partnership that he had taken all the way to his heart had affected her in some way.

Tinnin's sigh was audible and he lifted his spur, the one that perpetually sat on his desk, and spun the rowel absently. "When this is all settled, the tribe would like to offer you a position."

"Auto pool?" he asked, trying not to feel insulted. It was considerate of them to think at all about his future because the market for fast cars by the Wolf Posse had just dried up.

Thank goodness and heck, yeah, he thought.

"No," said Bear Den. "With the tribal council and in conjunction with our school system. They want you as a youth counselor."

"A what?" His head snapped up and he looked from one man to the next. They did not smirk and nothing in their expressions indicated that they were pulling his leg.

"I don't have any qualifications for that," he said.

"We disagree. You are overqualified to work with troubled kids and we have more than most," said Tinnin. "We'd consider it an honor to have you. And if you want some letters after your name, Kenshaw Little Falcon has offered to help you apply to the correct programs. Though I doubt they'll teach you anything you don't already know about human nature."

Ty stammered, "I—I don't know what to say."

It was a position of merit and respect. The very last sort of job he ever expected to be offered.

"Say yes," said Tinnin.

Chapter Twenty-Three

Beth waited with Hemi on the bottom step of Ty's place. She'd missed him this morning. Her black Escalade waited in his drive before the closed bay doors, packed and ready to go. Forrest had assured her that once this case was settled she'd have her pick of any field office in the country.

She was considering Phoenix. It wasn't New York, but it was a larger office than Oklahoma, though that no longer seemed to matter. She began to wonder if the real reason that she had wanted out of Oklahoma was that it was where her father had died. Perhaps some distance would help her come to terms with her mother's anger and allow them both to mend their relationship.

She'd called her mother today for the first time in she didn't know when. The conversation had been awkward, but it was a start.

Strange that, accidentally, while she was trying to solve a case, she had fallen in with a tribe and a family and a man who had all reminded her that family was worth fighting for. Ty had shown her what it felt like to be a part of something, and she wanted that. She loved it here. Turquoise Canyon was beautiful and, with all its flaws and troubles, it had people of character who loved this land and this tribe with the sort of selfless hearts she admired.

And Ty was here. If this was where he intended to be, then this was where she would stay, if he'd let her. He was worth losing a placement over. Why did she need to go to New York? The job here was no less valuable and neither the size of the field office nor the prestige of the placement made any difference to her now. She knew that because she'd finally gotten what she'd wanted and it didn't make her feel more important or more valuable.

She accepted in her heart that trying to be placed in an office of ex-army rangers and special ops agents would not bring her closer to her father any more than riding her bike or joining the army had done.

The offices in New York and DC handled big problems—global problems—and they were important. But so was this corner of the Southwest, so close to the Mexican border with all that that entailed.

The question remained, would Ty let her in?

The sound of the GTO's engine was unmistakable. Beth stood to greet Ty. Hemi rose and stretched, glancing back at her before trotting out to the road to escort Ty's gold Pontiac into his drive. He parked beside her Escalade, hands gripping the wheel as he glanced to her, and cut the engine. His expression was grim and his movements were slow as he exited the vehicle. Everything about him said he dreaded this meeting. Beth's heart sank and her smile dropped away.

He greeted Hemi with a pat and the dog trotted off to circle his Pontiac, sniffing as she went.

"Hey," Ty said.

"Hi there," she replied, forcing her hands into her back pockets, which caused her blazer to gape in the front so her shoulder holster and pistol showed.

She'd killed his father. The scene flashed before her, and her smile went brittle. What did he think of that?

Ty approached with a slow, measured tread.

"So, you all packed?" he asked, thumbing toward her vehicle. She was but not for the reasons he suspected.

She began to wonder what Forrest had told him. Did he know about her being called back to Oklahoma?

Ty continued without waiting for an answer. "You did it. Made a big case. Broke up the surrogate ring and took down our gang. Well done, Agent Hoosay."

"We don't have all your girls back yet. Still working on that."

"You think you'll find them?" he asked.

His gaze slipped over her and she felt her body responding to just his glance. She held herself back, not wanting to make a mistake. This was too important. "I have confidence that their location will come to light. I'm not going to give up."

"That's good."

He wasn't looking at her now and it seemed he was trying not to look at her.

"Ty?" she asked. She drew her hands from her pockets and intended for them to hang at her sides but found herself reaching for him. "I have to go to Oklahoma for a while. But it's temporary."

"Before you get your promotion?"

"Yes, but I'd call it a choice of placements."

"I remember. DC or NYC. All the important initials." Ty's shoulder throbbed. His heart ached and he could not keep himself from staring at her. She was going without him, onward and upward, to take on the world. And he would stay here and protect his tiny corner of it. "Congratulations, Agent Hoosay. I'm happy for you."

How had he even managed to say that? *Happy for her?* He needed to get away before he did something unforgivable, like begging her to stay here. He glanced at his garage and the tiny apartment above, feeling all his insecurities roiling up like the river after the monsoon.

She reached and took hold of him by each hand, her cold palms sliding into his warmer ones. "Are you? I was hoping you'd want me to stay."

He blinked at her. "Stay? Stay where?"

Hemi returned and nosed at their joined hands. Beth laughed and released one hand to pet Hemi's blockish head.

"Ty, I don't want to leave you. If you let me, I'll transfer to the office in Phoenix or Flagstaff so this would be my territory." She motioned to the world around them.

"Here? You want to stay here? That doesn't make any sense," he said, but his heart was hammering now, crashing against his ribs like a fist. "Why would you do that?"

"To be with you."

He withdrew his hand from hers and stepped back. "No. You are not giving up everything you've worked for to stay here."

"Why not?"

"Because you'll resent me for it, for making you lose your chance."

"First, I wouldn't have a chance if you hadn't helped me because we both know I had exactly zero likelihood to make this case alone. Second, I love it here. Your tribe is special, Ty. You're special."

"You're making a mistake," he said.

"No mistake. I love you, Ty, and I will do anything and everything to prove it."

"I don't want you here."

She gave him a knowing smile. "Yeah, right. Not this time, buddy."

He shook his head, not understanding what she meant.

"You think love is selfless. You sacrificed for your family, to keep your brothers safe, to give them families of their own, and you did all that at your own expense. How about I show you the kind of love that does not require loss? My love for you will make us stronger and it won't hurt."

He swallowed past the lump.

"Are you sure?" he whispered.

Beth stepped into his arms and wrapped her hands about his neck, kissing him on the lips. When she drew back, he was certain that he wondered if she might really mean it.

"I'm yours, Ty Redhorse. I've found the best man for me and you know I am not letting you go. I love you, Ty."

He gathered her against his chest, resting his cheek on the top of her head.

"Thank God," he whispered.

Epilogue

Two months passed, and January arrived with a cold, constant rain. Here in Atlanta, Georgia, the winter was wet and gray. The raid had been successful. Ty and Beth stood together outside the adults-only establishment in FBI rain slickers. The puddles and wet pavement reflected the flashing neon pink of the sign that read: *Girls All Nude* and the red and blue lights of the police cruisers.

The local FBI field agents brought out the entertainers one by one. Beside Ty stood his brother Colt and Colt's wife, Kacey. The arrest of Victor Vitoli and his crew had led to the capture of Leonard Usov himself. Usov was the head of the western territory for the Kuznetsov crime organization. Kostya Kuznetsov himself was in custody and Ty trusted Beth's assessment that the crime boss would not be wriggling out of the charges against him.

Both Maggie Kesselman and Brenda Espinoza had been recovered in December from a surrogate house outside Tucson, both pregnant. They were two of many recovered just days after a raid spearheaded by Luke Forrest based on intel from the materials and files recovered during the Turquoise Canyon rez case.

Forrest had given Beth a courtesy call so Kacey Doka Redhorse and Colt could be on hand for the recovery of Kacey's best friend. With Usov and Vitoli behind bars, there was no need to continue their witness protection. The young couple had elected to come home immediately with their son, Charlie.

Chief Wallace Tinnin had come with them along with their tribe's psychologist and medicine man, Kenshaw Little Falcon. Tinnin wore a tribal police jacket and Kenshaw stood in a saturated sheepskin jacket, more appropriate for the mountains of Arizona. The wide brims of their cowboy hats kept the rain from their faces.

The back door of the building banged open. A group of three more women emerged, their eyes wide and frightened. Some of the employees here were legitimate, but many were human slaves, sold to this establishment by the Kuznetsov organization. Here they worked as servers, dancers and prostitutes, never leaving the property. Ty wondered how Faras would feel at seeing them at the moment of their release, thin, hunched and defeated. The shame wafted from them like a living thing. Ty grieved at witnessing their suffering.

Beside him, Kacey gave a shout. Then she called out, "Marta!"

The last girl in the group turned. Her once lovely brown skin had taken on yellowish undertones and there were dark circles beneath her eyes. But Ty knew her. That was Marta Garcia, Kacey's dearest friend and the last of their women to be recovered.

Marta's eyes widened and her hands came to her mouth. Tears sprang from her eyes. Kacey ran the distance to her friend. The two embraced, sobbing, as they dropped to their knees in the parking lot in the rain.

Ty swallowed down the lump in his throat at witnessing their reunion. He hoped that the tribe would follow through with their decision to turn all members of the Wolf Posse over to state authorities for prosecution with the exception of Randy Tasa. He was glad that Detective Bear Den had agreed to foster Randy. With that sort of role model in his life, the boy would have a chance.

Forrest stepped up beside Ty.

"What will happen to Marta's baby?" asked Ty.

He knew from Beth that they had found the names of all the birth parents who had donated sperm and paid exorbitant fees for the care of their surrogates without knowing that the photos and reports they received were all bogus. Their surrogates were not happy, smart college grad students funding their education through surrogacy. They were slaves.

"Courts will have to decide. There will be repercussions."

"You mean fines?"

"Definitely. Perhaps criminal charges. They've broken the law by not using the legitimate options available to them. I don't know if the state will take away their children. They're the genetic parents, but…" Forrest rubbed his neck. "I'm glad I don't have to sort that all out."

Colt left them to go to his wife and her friend. He wrapped a blanket about Marta's shoulders and Kacey helped her rise.

"You're going home with us, Marta. It's over now," said Kacey.

Marta clung and nodded. Ty thought it would not be over for the victims for quite some time. Such abuse left damage. But he knew that Kenshaw had put together a mental health team to help the returned deal with their emotional trauma. Just as he had helped his mom in the aftermath of the shooting.

Perhaps the women who had been taken would find some comfort in knowing that no other among them would suffer what they had gone through because of the work of the good people of their tribe.

"You ready to go home, Ty?" Beth asked.

Her transfer had been approved and she now worked out of the FBI field office in Phoenix, Arizona. He nodded and took her hand and they headed back toward the waiting vehicles, getting out of the way and letting the locals take care of business.

THE WOLF POSSE was crushed. Ty and Beth would be two of many who would make sure that it would not rise from the dust. But first they had a wedding to plan and a house to build.

"I've been thinking of buying some horses," she said.

"Barrel racing?" he asked.

"Yeah. For a start."

"Sounds good."

What a joy to be able to do what she loved with the man she adored, a man who knew better than most about risk and reward.

They walked together, arm in arm.

"I'm glad you feel that way," she said.

"Beth, I love riding horses and our bikes, but more than anything, I love you."

She smiled. "Don't let Hemi hear you say that."

"No." He laughed. "I won't."

Beth paused before him and then leaned in to kiss him on the lips. When she drew back she rested her hands on his chest.

"I love you, Ty."

* * * * *

#1791 BODY OF EVIDENCE
Colby Agency: Sexi-ER • by Debra Webb
When Dr. Marissa Frasier wakes up in bed next to her dead ex-husband, she turns to Lacon Traynor, one of the Colby Agency's best investigators, for help. In Lacon's protective arms, Marissa feels safe...but is the murderer closer than she imagines?

#1792 SAVED BY THE SHERIFF
Eagle Mountain Murder Mystery • by Cindi Myers
Three years after Sheriff Travis Walker sent Lacy Milligan to prison for murder, he's uncovered evidence that clears Lacy's name. Now the former enemies must work together to find the real killer—and time may be running out.

#1793 SWAT STANDOFF
Tennessee SWAT • by Lena Diaz
Partners Blake Sullivan and Donna Waters must put aside their differences and work together when the rest of their SWAT team is kidnapped. Sparks fly between them, but will they be able to find their teammates before it's lights out?

#1794 MAJOR CRIMES
Omega Sector: Under Siege • by Janie Crouch
Four years ago Cain Bennett ensured Hayley Green's arrest, and he's lived with the guilt of his former lover's incarceration ever since. Now, though, the people she was once trying to expose are after her—and only Cain can keep her safe.

#1795 RANGER GUARDIAN
Texas Brothers of Company B • by Angi Morgan
Texas Ranger Heath Murray and FBI agent Kendall Barlow must hunt down their daughter's kidnapper. But as they race against time, will they get a second chance at love?

#1796 RULES IN BLACKMAIL
by Nichole Severn
Someone is stalking prosecutor Jane Reise, and she knows she needs the help of irresistible former navy SEAL Sullivan Bishop. A tense shared history has him shutting her out, so she's forced to blackmail him. As her stalker closes in, they'll put their lives—and their hearts—on the line.

YOU CAN FIND MORE INFORMATION ON UPCOMING HARLEQUIN® TITLES, FREE EXCERPTS AND MORE AT WWW.HARLEQUIN.COM.

HICNM0618

Get 4 **FREE REWARDS!**

We'll send you 2 FREE Books <u>plus</u> 2 FREE Mystery Gifts.

Harlequin® Intrigue books feature heroes and heroines that confront and survive danger while finding themselves irresistibly drawn to one another.

FREE Value Over **$20**

"What are you saying? That instead of accepting that they could
be lost in the woods, you think someone came up here and…what?
What did he do with them?"

"No, I'm not saying that at all. I'm just throwing out the facts
as we know them. The team drove up but didn't drive back down.
They aren't answering their phones, radios or us yelling at the top
of our lungs. Something bad must have happened."

Her voice was barely above a whisper the next time she spoke.
"I think we may be in over our heads. We should call the station,
get some volunteers out here to help us conduct a more thorough
search. Even if they're not lost, they could be stranded somewhere,
maybe in a cell phone and radio dead zone. Obviously something
happened to them or their vehicles wouldn't still be here."

"Agreed. We need to get some help out here."

He raised his flashlight beam, training it straight ahead, slicing a
path of light through the darkness of trees and bushes about twenty
feet away. "While you make that call, I'm going to go deeper in
to check that barn and the clearing in front of it. There have to
be some footprints there, maybe a piece of torn fabric caught on
a branch. I'd like to find some tangible proof that might show us
where the team was last. The trackers will want to start from the
last known position."

She shoved her cell phone back into her pocket. "We're not splitting up. I'm your partner. We'll check it out together. Then I'll call this in."

The wobble in her voice had him hesitating. He looked down at her, noted the intensity in her expression, the shine of unshed tears sparkling in her eyes. He'd been with Destiny PD since late fall of the previous year and had been her partner for over four months. In all that time, she'd always been decisive, in control, never breaking down no matter how tough things got. He'd never once seen her rattled. But right now she seemed…fragile, vulnerable. And he'd bet it wasn't just because she was worried about her friends. There was something else going on here. And he thought he knew what it was.

"Donna?"

"Yeah?"

"It's not your fault."

She frowned. "What's not my fault?"

"Whatever happened, whatever is going on with the team. I think you're second-guessing yourself, feeling guilty. But if anyone's to blame, it's me. If I'd been a good partner to you, we'd have both been here with them when—"

"When what? When aliens beamed them up to the mother ship? Come on, Blake. This is crazy. Four highly trained SWAT team members and the chief of police don't just disappear off the face of the earth. You know what I'm starting to think is going on? Group hysteria, or mass hysteria, or whatever psychologists call it. We're both feeding off each other's fears and making this into something it's not."

"I honestly hope you're right."

See what happens next when SWAT STANDOFF by award-winning author Lena Diaz goes on sale in June 2018 wherever Harlequin Intrigue books are sold!

www.Harlequin.com

Need an adrenaline rush from nail-biting tales
(and irresistible males)?

Check out **Harlequin® Intrigue®**
and **Harlequin® Romantic Suspense** books!

New books available every month!

CONNECT WITH US AT:

Harlequin.com/Community

 Facebook.com/HarlequinBooks

Twitter.com/HarlequinBooks

Instagram.com/HarlequinBooks

Pinterest.com/HarlequinBooks

ReaderService.com

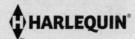

**ROMANCE WHEN
YOU NEED IT**

THE WORLD IS BETTER WITH

Romance

Harlequin has everything from contemporary, passionate and heartwarming to suspenseful and inspirational stories.

Whatever your mood, we have a romance just for you!

Connect with us to find your next great read, special offers and more.

f /HarlequinBooks

🐦 @HarlequinBooks

www.HarlequinBlog.com

www.Harlequin.com/Newsletters

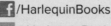
⊕ HARLEQUIN®

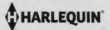
Romance FOR EVERY MOOD™

www.Harlequin.com

SERIESHALOAD2015

SCGENRE2017